CHINA DREAMS

BY

IRENE MAHONEY, O.S.U.

AuthorHouse™
1663 Liberty Drive
Bloomington, IN 47403
www.authorhouse.com
Phone: 1-800-839-8640

Published by AuthorHouse 05/08/2012

ISBN: 978-1-4772-0257-9 (sc)
ISBN: 978-1-4772-0258-6 (e)

This book is printed on acid-free paper.

OTHER BOOKS BY IRENE MAHONEY

Marie of the Incarnation: Mystic and Missionary

Royal Cousin: The Life of Henri of Navarre

Madame Catherine: The Life of Catherine de Medici

Seven Sons

Accidental Grace

Marie of the Incarnation: Selected Writings

Far from Home

A Company of Women

Swatow: Ursulines in China

A Far Country

Lady Blackrobes

Encounters: A Book of Memories

Solo Voices: A Novel of Forgiveness

PLAYS

Portraits of Angela

All That I Am

Not by Half

Off With Their Heads

ACKNOWLEDGEMENTS

This is the third time that I have had the opportunity of working with the staff of Authorhouse. In every case I have found the experience more than satisfying. From beginning to end the staff has been understanding, competent, helpful, available. What could have been difficult moments they managed with ease and grace. I am grateful to each of them.

It is also the third time that I have experienced the good fortune of working with Theresa Eppridge, O.S.U. and Marie-Celine Miranda, O.S.U.: Marie-Celine as my diligent proofreader and Theresa as my imaginative graphic designer. Her cover design, I have found, is the perfect symbol for drawing the reader into *China Dreams.*

It is, however, Ellen Mary Mylod, O.S.U. to whom I owe my understanding of the material on which *China Dreams* is based. She was waiting for me on that bright sunny afternoon when I stepped off the train from Taipei and she never left me in the years that followed. She interpreted words, explained customs, solaced my loneliness. Bewildered by responses which often seemed to me to defy meaning, I leaned on Ellen's sure and steady understanding of a culture which I found both alien and alluring. Whatever I know of China dreams I know because I have been taught by a master.

TO ALICE GALLIN, O.S.U.

Treasured Colleague

Trusted Friend

EPIGRAPH

COME, THEY SAID, LET US MAKE A CITY AND A TOWER,
THE TOP OF WHICH MAY REACH TO HEAVEN.
AND LET US MAKE OUR NAME FAMOUS.
BUT GOD CONFOUNDED THEIR TONGUE
SO THAT THEY NO LONGER UNDERSTOOD ONE
ANOTHER'S SPEECH
AND THEY WERE SCATTERED FROM THAT PLACE INTO
MANY LANDS.

GENESIS 11

CONTENTS

CHINA DREAMS

PROLOGUE

Chen Shang-Li slept well but he was stiff when he woke. It wasn't the damp; he was used to that. And now it was almost summer and the weather was warm. He was getting old; he knew it yesterday as he herded his ducks across the fields. He was tired long before the sun set. He had slept in the shadow of a large school building by the side of a rice field. He always recognized the big sign: Ho-Ping. You could see it from far off. He could not read very well but he know these characters meant "Harmony". It was quiet and safe with no one to bother him provided he got on his way with the first light before the cooks were up to fix rice for the students.

The mist was still heavy but he could see the shadowy wings of the great white cranes hovering over the rice field. His ducks were already awake, pecking here and there amid the stubble. It was still too dark to count them but he didn't worry; in all the years he had been herding, he had never lost a single bird. That was why he could still get hired. They knew that even though he was an old man he could be trusted to know his business. He picked up his staff and clucked softly, softly, so he wouldn't disturb anyone who might be awake. He should reach the market by late afternoon. It took him longer now, three days instead of two, but no matter, he would get there with his flock safe and sound. It was better to go slow, as he always explained; it gave the ducks more time to eat along the way so they would be fatter when they reached the market.

They waddled ahead of him, pecking here and there, in

no special order, but always keeping close together. The mist had begun to lift a little but when he looked back at the school there were still no lights on. He wondered what it would be like always to live indoors, going to bed each night on the same bed, fixing the same pot for rice each morning. He could see quite a bit ahead of him now. As the ducks passed the water-tower toward the end of the school property, he noticed that they were fanning out into two groups as though they were avoiding something in their path.

He peered ahead. At first he could see nothing but then he made out a little mound on the grass. When he came closer he saw that it was a piece of clothing. Perhaps a jacket or a coat if he were lucky. He didn't need it for himself but if it were in good condition he could easily sell it. But when he came abreast of it he saw that it was more than a jacket–beyond the heap of material a leg extended, a woman's leg without a shoe. He looked at it, bewildered, for a few seconds, before he realized that the ducks were moving on. He straightened up, walking as fast as he could to head them off, using his staff to signal them to stay still.

By the time he had circled around them, he was a little out of breath and he stopped for a moment before walking back toward the body. By this time the light was much stronger and he could see that it was a young girl and that very clearly she was dead. She was lying on her face, her thick black hair coming almost to her waist. Thank the Lord of Heaven for that. It would be terrible to look upon the face of the dead. Even so he was frightened and he pulled back, looking toward the school to see if there was any movement.

It was a young body, he could tell. And she was not poor. Her clothing was of good quality, wrinkled now and wet from the dew but of good quality just the same. It was a puzzle to find her here. Once when he was young and the armies were fighting there were bodies like this everywhere–but not any more. Perhaps a man had killed her–used her and then killed her. Such things happened often now when girls went here and there on their big feet, alone, with no one to protect them. Despite his fear he looked more closely. One arm was stretched out beyond the body and there was a ring on the finger. Perhaps she had been married or promised in marriage. But why would a man leave her here, so openly, without bush or tree to hide the body? He looked again. The ring looked to be of good quality, gold perhaps. It would bring a good price; but he could not bring himself to touch the body. Terrible luck might follow him for the rest of his life. Bad enough that he had come so close.

He straightened up and once again looked back toward the school. He hoped no one had seen him. There was no telling what they might accuse him of. He picked up his staff and clucked at the ducks. They started moving forward and as he turned to follow, there before him was a shoe. It was a fine shoe, black and of good stuff. He turned it over and weighed it in his hand. The sole was hardly worn. Since it had turned up straight in front of him, it seemed clear that it was meant to be his. But one shoe? Even one fine shoe? Who would buy it? He turned back toward the body, shuddering a little as he realized he would have to touch it, even move it a bit, if he were to get the second shoe. He hesitated; the light was full now and he could see the broken body very clearly. His teeth clamped tight with fear but the shoe in his hand moved him to action.

He knelt by the body, pushing it so that it lay on its side. Carefully he averted his eyes so that he would not see the face. The leg was crumpled and the jagged bone pierced through the stocking. He pulled the short skirt down as far as he could and yanked at the shoe. It came off at once and he shoved it into his knapsack next to its mate.

As he looked back once more toward the school, he thought he saw a light in the basement but that was all. He caught up with the ducks, guiding them into a little diagonal path that would lead to another set of fields. He looked at his hands and rubbed them hard against his pants. He had touched the dead. He rubbed them again, wetting his lips against his fear. At the first pond he would wash them, wash them hard, and when he went to sell the shoes he would take them from his bag with a piece of old paper so that he would never touch them again. He would have liked to polish them a little, make them look more valuable; they were dull from the dew on the grass. But it wasn't worth the risk; he had touched them enough. You couldn't be too careful about bad luck.

1

The Saturday morning my brother called I was fixing an early breakfast so I could help chaperone an art class for their museum trip to the Cloisters.

"Les, it's Tom. I'm out here at Kennedy."

"Kennedy!" I couldn't believe it.

"Right. I just got in on a flight from Tokyo."

"What's the matter? Are you OK?" I figured he must be sick; he wasn't due home until July–another three weeks.

"I'm fine. A little spacey from the trip but otherwise in good shape. The Taipei deal fell through. A real certified mess. There wasn't any point in keeping me out there so they decided to send me back to the Home Office to sort things out. Listen, I'm going to take a taxi; I've got too much luggage to manage on the bus. Wait till you see your wedding present. Confucius say: Beautiful present for lovely bride."

The spiral of joy his voice had stirred in me zigzagged out of control and plummeted down. My letter must have just missed him. There was no point in trying to explain on the phone. He'd know soon enough.

"Tom, look, I'm not going to be home this morning. I promised to help our art teacher on a museum trip but I'll be home early this afternoon. Mom and Pop are still asleep but I'll run up and tell them you're coming in."

"No, don't do that. Let me surprise them. Whoops! My time's run out and I don't have any more American change. OK, see you soon, Les." And he hung up.

It was after three when I got home that afternoon but Mom and Pop and Tom were still sitting around the kitchen table. It was clear that I was the subject of the conversation. Tom was leaning back in his chair, his arms locked behind his head, his legs stretched out.

For the first time in my life I dreaded seeing him. Neither of us had gone away to college and it wasn't until Tom had taken a job that kept him traveling a good bit of the time that we were separated. His homecomings had always been my happiest hours, filled with that special affection shared between twins. But now I was filled with what? Dread? Fear? Shame? When he came over and put his arms around me, none of the silly little hugs and pushes that dated from our childhood worked. I was stiff in his arms. I could feel it but I couldn't control it.

Pop had moved his chair over and Mom had started to set another place.

"Doesn't your brother look wonderful?" she said.

I stood back from him and met his eyes. "Wonderful. I thought maybe his eyes would have started to slant after all that time in the exotic Orient."

Tom smiled. "Only at night. Come on, Les, sit down."

"Your mother made us Welsh rarebit," Pop said. "She can heat some up for you."

"That's OK; never mind. I had a hot dog with the kids."

"Are you sure, Leslie? How about some coffee? I can

make some hot." Mom had begun to bustle.

"That's all right, Mom, this is fine."

"Then why don't you two go into the living room. I'm going to clear up out here and your father wants to go and wash the car." It was clearly a new idea to Pop but he took Mom's lead. She was doing her best to see that we would be alone together.

We sat in the living room, Tom and I, and made conversation. How was Hong Kong? Was it really the most fabulous shopping center in the world? Did he learn Chinese? How come he never went to the Mainland? What did he do in Taiwan? What was the food like? Did he learn to use chopsticks?

Tom sat in Pop's old rocker with a hassock under his feet and I curled up on the couch, my shoes off and my feet tucked under me. They were our old postures; we had gone to them like homing pigeons. Just like old times. Except that now my part of that spacious inner world we had always shared was walled and barred. Not open, even to Tom.

Once when I looked over I saw Tom nodding. He came to with a start.

"God, Les, I'm sorry. What a terrible thing to do when I've just gotten home."

"You must be dead."

"Body clock's off. Let's see, it would be just about 4:00 a.m. in Hong Kong now."

"Go up and take a nap. I might take one myself. It's been a tough day. Twenty kids lassoed into a medieval museum on a gorgeous Saturday. What torture!" Tom got up, pushing the hassock back into place. I leaned down to put my shoes on and when I stood up Tom was in front of me, reaching out to take my hands.

"I got your letter," he said. "I don't understand what's going on, Les, but you know I want to help any way I can."

I shrugged. "I broke off my engagement with Hal; that's what's going on."

Tom was floundering, trying to catch my tone. I hated what I was doing to him. He looked so beat and so bewildered. More than anything in the world I wanted to put my arms around him and tell him I was OK, that I was sure the break with Hal–painful as it was–had been the right thing to do.

"Les." Tom had put his hands on my shoulders and the pressure was wonderfully comforting. "Look, Les. You don't have to talk. You don't have to say anything until you're ready. It's just hard watching you like this and not being able to help."

I nodded. I didn't look up. I couldn't risk it.

Hal and I had been dating since our sophomore year in college. Maybe that was the trouble. It had all been so easy. While my friends dated, broke up, wept a few tears, dated again, Hal and I danced on. At Christmas, on my third year out of college, we had announced our engagement to no one's surprise. And one week later, on New Year's Eve, I found him on the club patio with Renata Driscoll.

Hal, of course, assured me that it meant nothing–a moment of New Year's Eve exuberance. He loved me; surely I could not doubt it after all this time. And, in fact,

I didn't. So when he assured me it meant nothing to him, I knew it was true. But as the weeks passed it was just this that upset me. So many things I began to see that were so important to me Hal could dismiss with a shrug and that engaging smile. Was this how our marriage was going to be? Hal brushing aside as incidental what to me demanded our consideration? When I told him I did not want to go through with our marriage, he was surprised but not destroyed–and I knew I had made the right decision.

Fortunately, from the beginning we had planned a simple wedding and there were few preparations to be undone. My explanation to my parents was certainly insufficient but with their usual good grace they accepted my tight-lipped reasoning.

Sunday Tom spent part of the day sleeping and I stayed in my room correcting a final set of examinations. I was relieved when Monday came and I could leave early for school.

Whitfield Academy had been my first teaching assignment and it had been a perfect place for me–small, private, and with a class of students that generally precluded discipline problems. Even so the last weeks of school were always tumultuous. Tests were over and the weather was already oppressively warm. The kids were filled with that peculiar restless energy which made them accident-prone. They tripped over wastebaskets, dropped book-ends on each other's toes, giggled hysterically, broke vases and then cut themselves on the shards of glass as they tried to clean up. Everything blew out of proportion and the days seemed endless.

Even had my own life been on a more even keel they

would have been difficult days, but as it was they seemed almost unbearable. When, finally, I closed the classroom door and started walking to the subway, I was close to tears. For a moment I thought the man walking down the subway stairs just ahead of me was Hal. It was the last straw and when I got home I went straight to bed with a sick headache. Mom brought up beef bouillon and saltines–the panacea for all ills–and when I finished I turned off my light. It would keep Tom from knocking, I thought.

Despite two aspirin I slept badly and when I got up in the morning my head still ached. School was a nightmare. I was dizzy and light-headed, I yelled at the kids, and lost the key to the supply room. Seven more days, I kept telling myself; just seven more days and school would be over.

I had never made close friends with any of the faculty. Most of them were older than I and relationships were generally kept on a professional basis. Aside from vague references about a change in my plans I had said little about my broken engagement. They were all much too polite to question me but even so I found it hard to sustain the chatter of the cafeteria. At noon I decided to go to the teachers' room where I could get a quiet cup of tea. On the way I passed the Head Mistress's office and she waved to me from her desk.

"Did the key to the supply closet turn up?" she asked as I approached her door.

"Oh, yes, of course. Right on the edge of my desk," I answered.

"Certainly, just where you had looked a dozen times," she laughed.

I liked Miss Baker. She had a wisdom and a directness that made it easy for her faculty to work with her.

She pushed the papers to the side of her desk and nodded toward me. "Do you have a minute? I like to chat with my faculty before the end of term. Find out what exotic vacations they're planning. Miss Bridge is going to Iceland, she tells me–lucky lady. And what about you, Leslie?"

Miss Baker always called us by our formal names and I was surprised and taken off my guard. Suddenly the summer rose before me, empty and unplanned. Now, hardly aware that I had made a decision, I smiled and took the chair by her desk and found myself telling her of my broken engagement. She nodded but made no comment. And I found myself plunging into the tangle of mingled emotions I had hidden even from myself.

"I've always loved it here at Whitfield," I said, "but right now . . . . " I lifted my hands helplessly. "I know life has to go on and all that but I wish it could go on somewhere else."

I stopped, bewildered at this unexpected outpouring, but Miss Baker looked neither surprised nor embarrassed. "What might help, do you think?" she asked. "I know you have found teaching very demanding this semester. Would you like some time off? I could easily arrange a semester's leave with the option of returning for the spring semester."

I shook my head. "I don't think so," I said. "Teaching is really good for me; it takes me out of myself. Maybe I just need to be in a different place."

"Well, then," Miss Baker was smiling, "How about some

overseas teaching?"

"Overseas?" I had never thought of such a thing. "Like where?"

"Well, that we would have to work out. But I'm sure you are aware that everyone these days wants to learn English, especially from native speakers. And since language arts is your specialty you have an edge on the market."

I floundered for something to say. "I guess I never thought . . . ."

"Leslie, dear, the last thing I ever meant was to push you into something . . . ."

I cut her off at once. "Oh, no, Miss Baker. Really it sounds wonderful. I guess I'm just sort of blown out of the water, as the kids say."

She laughed. "Well, think about it if it appeals; if not, don't give it a second thought. Maybe I was just projecting my dreams on you. I have always wanted to live abroad for more than just a vacation. So far I haven't had the opportunity." She reached over and pulled a file from her drawer. "Here are a few possibilities," she said as she handed me a number of catalogs. "Lots of pretty pictures, if nothing else. I think you'll find them interesting. If anything appeals let me know and I will see what I can do."

Altogether I had spent no more than a half-hour in Miss Baker's office but when I left I was energized. For the first time in weeks I felt that I was acting–doing something instead of letting life harry me. There was no one in the teachers' room and I picked up the phone and dialed home. I was lucky. Tom answered.

"Tom, it's Les. What are you doing this afternoon? No, that's OK. Go to the dentist but then can you meet me at the Botanical Gardens? Yes, the main entrance, the one we always use. I can be there by 3:30. And Tom, tell Mom we'll get something to eat while we're out. OK? I'll see you at 3:30." For the first time in months the walk to the subway was not a drag.

Tom was waiting for me at the gate. We walked down the path between the Japanese cherry trees and sat on a bench near the rock garden. There were some kids playing off on the hillside but otherwise we had the place to ourselves.

Tom stretched out his legs waiting for me to say something and when I didn't he looked at me quizzically but asked no questions.

Finally I said, "I just cancelled my contract for next year."

His only response was a more quizzical look. "That's it?"

I shrugged. "I need a change."

"Like what?"

I groped. "I don't know; I have to work it out."

Tom had turned away and was looking out over the garden, squinting into the sun.

The silence between us was becoming uncomfortable.

Finally I said, "Tom, I have to get away. I can't cope with people gossiping and trying to figure out what happened between me and Hal. Even Mom and Pop are just making it harder."

"They love you."

"I know. That's what makes it so hard."

He sighed. "So what do you have in mind?"

"I didn't have anything in mind until I started to talk with Miss Baker at Whitfield and she gave me all this stuff about overseas teaching." And I began rummaging about in my tote bag. "Don't they look fascinating?" and I spread out the brochures on my lap.

"I imagine they look fascinating to a lot of people," Tom said sceptically. "You better get a move on if you expect to get one of these assignments. I suspect you'll find that there are dozens of Ph.D.s with university affiliations trying for cushy little international posts for a year or two."

Tom, as it turned out, was discouragingly right. Many of the deadlines I had already missed and others demanded qualifications that I lacked. By the beginning of August I had begun to think my dream was hopeless.

"You haven't tried some of the less desirable places."

"Like what? Africa or Mongolia?"

Tom laughed."Not quite. I can't see you in darkest Africa."

"Where then?"

He had no immediate answer and "where then" was where we left it until one hot afternoon Tom knocked on my door, waving an e-mail.

"I think I have something of interest. I have been secretly working behind your back and I think we have a possible overseas assignment."

While he was in Taipei, Tom explained, he had met up with a guy who had been at the university with him. "Maybe you remember him," he suggested. "Vince Grogan?"

"Sure. Basketball player at the university. You brought him over to the house for dinner a couple of times. I kept waiting for him to ask me out and then I found out he was planning to be a priest."

Tom nodded. "He's out in Taiwan now on a missionary service assignment. I saw a good bit of him while I was in Taipei. He works with students in one of the universities. Seemed like he might have some interesting leads so since nothing else had turned up for you I sent him an e-mail, explaining what you were after and *voila*! here we have an answer."

Yes, Vince did have the name of a school which was looking for a native English speaker to teach the fourth and fifth level in a junior college. It was situated in a rural district several hours south of Taipei. The name of the college was Ho-Ping situated in the city of Chi-Yi.

"Tell Leslie," the e-mail continued, "that if she is interested she should send them her college transcript, letters from her principal and head of department and anything else–prizes, grants, awards–that makes her look important. Or if she prefers she can send everything to me and I will be happy to deliver it."

The news left me speechless. It was one thing to dream the impossible dream but Vincent's information was something else. Tom was looking at me, his lips pursed. "Look, Les, you don't have to go on with this, you know. You don't have to try to win the Purple Heart."

But as he spoke, my initial hesitation spiraled into a movement of confidence. My life was beginning again. I wasn't groveling, waiting for the blows to fall. I was in charge. I reached out and hugged Tom.

"It's OK," I said. "It's going to be fine."

11

On September 8, just three months since I had tendered my resignation and said farewell to Whitfield Academy, I arrived at Taipei's Chiang Kai-Shek International Airport.

Except for a few hours during our stop-over in Anchorage the flight had been in darkness. Although I had armed myself with a mystery novel and a folder of crossword puzzles, I was too tired, too distracted to do either. I kept falling asleep, then waking with a jerk, my neck stiff, my mouth dry, my eyes sandy. The Chinese gentleman in the window seat next to me did not share my discomfort. He slept soundly, his shoes off, a pillow behind his head, the gold rings on his fingers catching the light from the overhead bulb. But as we neared Taipei he was immediately alert: shoes, tie, jacket all instantly in place.

"Goodbye," he said, bowing to me, "Come again."

But by the time I had made my way to Immigration and Customs I decided that if I lived through this time I would never, never come again. I was not only cross-eyed with fatigue but I clearly was lacking in Oriental assertiveness training. By the time I collected my suitcases most of the luggage wagons were gone and I was left guiding one with a badly crippled back wheel. Seeing an elegantly dressed Indian with only one small valise, I trundled into place behind him. But it soon became clear that my decision was poorly made. As he approached the Customs booth he turned suddenly and clapped his hands. At once his small be-saried wife and four docile children, each lugging a suitcase, ranged themselves politely behind their father–and in front of me.

When, at last, I emerged from Customs and Immigration I felt tousled and wrinkled–and, by comparison, very large. The blue knit dress which had seemed so appropriate for traveling was rumpled and stained from my inept use of chopsticks on the plane and my hair felt damp and unkempt on my neck. At least, I thought, if Vincent is waiting to meet me as he promised, there will be no problem of recognition. Nor was there. Even among the crowds that poured in and out of the airport, Vincent Grogan was clearly visible: tall, lean, blond, a little stooped.

"Leslie, welcome to Taiwan. Here let me take those," and he hoisted up my two suitcases. "You're probably staggering with fatigue." I nodded, hardly able to answer. The heat and noise of the street had taken my breath away.

"This way," he directed. "Here." He put my luggage on the sidewalk and motioned to a taxi. "Ordinarily I use my Honda but I figured we'd do better with a taxi tonight." He pushed me in and heaved my suitcases in after me.

The ride from the airport took about forty-five minutes–forty-five minutes of mingled sensations as I looked about me: the listing telephone poles and the wires looping crazily over the roadways, swinging so low that it seemed that a tall person might possibly be electrocuted by them; the smells of open sewers, of a million kinds of unknown foods; and of that pervasive smell that I was soon to discover penetrated everything–the smell of ginger.

It was too dark to see much but what I saw destroyed my myth of beautiful Chinese design. There were no pagodas, none of the graceful tiled roofs I had associated with Chinese architecture. Instead there were rows of square little concrete boxes, shaped like bunkers. Or larger shapes, apartment buildings of five or six floors, all constructed with the same graceless concrete and in the same graceless style.

Vendors pushed their carts everywhere but unlike the vendors of Mexico (the only other country I had ever visited) there were no bright colors, no pyramids of oranges or mangoes turning pink in the sunshine. It seemed to me on that first night that if I were to die in Taiwan, it would be not from some dread Oriental disease but from simple ugliness.

"I wasn't sure," Vincent was saying, "what arrangements you wanted to make so I thought for tonight at least you could sleep in a little apartment we just bought. It's right next to our place so you won't feel too abandoned and in the morning you can come over for breakfast and we can plan your next step."

It was much darker now. We were out of the main part of the city, turning randomly into narrow little muddy lanes. The headlights of the car did nothing to disturb the crowds of children still playing in the street as the driver honked and yelled simultaneously. After several heated discussions between Vincent and the taxi driver–apparently on the subject of right and left–we finally stopped and Vincent got out.

"Here we are," he said and reached for my luggage. It was too dark to see where I was going and I swore as I stepped into a puddle that came up almost to my ankle.

"You OK?" Vincent asked.

CHAPTER II

"I just stepped in a puddle; it must have been raining."

"Not for the last two months," Vincent said and laughed. "Maybe you better take off your shoes before you come inside. Here, give them to me; I'll take care of them later."

That night I slept in a room as small as a closet. My bed was a wooden frame with a thin unyielding mattress covered with a bamboo mat. There was a single window and, of course, no screens. When the window was open, I could see bats swooping just beyond the panes. When it was closed, I thought I would suffocate. Open or closed the window did nothing to protect me from the noise of the adjoining apartments. Music wailed and pulsed on one side. Immediately above me a man and woman shouted for hours in Mandarin–that strange monosyllabic tongue which falls on Western ears like sharp and angry blows. Just before five o'clock I fell asleep. By that time Taipei was already on its feet, preparing for the strenuous business of living another day.

I woke with Vincent knocking on my door. "Sorry to do this to you, Leslie, but it's almost a quarter to ten and our water goes off at ten o'clock until late this evening. Precaution to avoid a drought. I thought you'd probably like a shower before you face the world."

I put my hand to my forehead. Not yet ten o'clock and already I was wet clear through. The shower was a tiny closet with spidery streams of water spraying in all directions but it was water and it was cool. I had no complaints.

That evening I met the other two members of Vincent's community: Father Paul, stooped and beetle-browed, a veteran of the Old China missions; and Bryan, young, red-faced and freckled, just back from his language studies in Chang-Hua. They were kind and hospitable, quick to get me a knife and fork when they noticed my unsuccessful efforts with chopsticks. But, even so, I felt ill at ease. They had a rhythm and style of life that didn't include a young American woman on her first Eastern journey.

After dinner Vincent mercifully suggested a walk. "It should have cooled down a little by now," he assured me, watching me wipe the sweat from the back of my neck. "Anyway, you'd probably be glad to get out of the house for a bit. I'm sorry no one was around this afternoon to show you about."

"No problem. I slept most of the day. I felt as though I were swimming under water."

"It happens to everybody. Don't forget, you're twelve hours ahead of yourself. Your body doesn't like it."

We had crossed the road and turned into another narrow lane, bordering a vast green field.

"Rice," Vincent explained. "Beautiful, isn't it? Perfect spring green."

It was beautiful, especially beautiful after the ugly little houses and the muddy lanes. As we watched, four large white birds rose vertically out of the rice and flew off against the sun.

"Your lucky day," Vincent congratulated me. "Cranes, symbols of good fortune."

The path had narrowed and we were walking single file. Despite the setting sun the heat had not appreciably diminished and a stillness, as dense as fog, had settled over us.

"Had enough?" Vincent asked, as I brushed the sweat away.

More than enough, I thought, as we turned back. Much more than enough. How am I going to do it? I wondered. How am I going to keep alive in this place? Maybe my brother had been right; maybe I would be home in three weeks.

"So," Vincent was saying, "there's no reason why you can't stay on with us until the weekend and then I'll be free to go with you to Chi-Yi. That would still give you time before college opens."

Today was only Tuesday. Three more days until Saturday. Three more days to spend in that tiny little room, senseless with sleep, three more days with nothing to do, waiting for Vincent to come home, to talk to me, take me for a walk, wake me out of my lethargy. I couldn't do it. I simply couldn't do it.

I thanked him. I told him how grateful I was, how nice it had been to have a place to stay, to meet his friends . . . but I thought it would be better to get on to Chi-Yi.

"You know you're welcome. I hope you don't think you're imposing."

No, I didn't think that. They had been wonderful, but . . . .

He looked at me and nodded. "I understand. We've all felt it when we've first come out. Dislocation. Nothing belongs to us. And we don't belong."

He had said it perfectly. Dislocation. I was an alien. Just as my visa so formally stated: a resident alien. I felt my throat tighten, but no tears came. Even they belonged to another world, a world that was no longer mine.

The next day, after lunch, I said goodbye to Father Paul and Bryan, and drove with Vincent to the railroad station. It was high noon and the station was mobbed. Against all regulations Vincent managed to push and shove himself past the gate and into the area for "Ticketed Passengers Only".

"Don't worry," he assured me, as he motioned me toward my reserved seat, "I've told the conductor to be sure to see that you get off at Chi-Yi and I'm going to leave your suitcases by the door. Somebody will help you with them. Call us tonight, if you can, and tell us how it went; and if there's anything I can do over the weekend just let us know. OK?"

He was off with a brush of a kiss on my cheek. I saw him push through the passenger gate just as they closed it and then he was out of sight. The conductor, it turned out, was a young woman, slight and trim in a navy blue uniform, with a voice easily heard over the rumble of the train. She eyed me carefully, examined my ticket front and back and then yelled "CHI-YI" at me several times. I nodded and she strode off returning with a pot of cold tea which she poured into a plastic glass. Another stern command was issued which I presumed meant, "Drink your tea!"

Thus began the final lap of my journey to Chi-Yi. Most of the three hours I spent rehearsing my interview with the president of the college. Vincent had been able to call him that morning to announce my arrival and had confirmed that I would be met at the railroad station. Dr. Liang, Vincent assured me, spoke excellent English. He was, in fact, a noted scholar who, before the Communist victory, had held a high post in a Beijing university. In Vincent's conversations with him he had indicated that he was delighted with my credentials and looked forward to having me on his faculty.

"There's another young woman teaching English there," Vincent had told me. "This will be her second year."

"An American?"

"I don't think so; English probably. Maybe someone whose family lives in Hong Kong. At any rate, Dr. Liang assures me that you can share an apartment with her until you get situated."

It seemed a rather arbitrary way of settling housing. "Suppose she doesn't want someone sharing an apartment?" I asked dubiously.

Vincent shrugged. "I imagine she'll be delighted. It doesn't have to be forever. You can always find your own place once you get the lay of the land."

"What's her name?" I asked.

"I don't know. Liang didn't say."

Well, at least, I thought, I'll have a place to stay tonight. At least that. Suddenly I was jerked from sleep, the conductor screaming at me, "Chi-Yi! Chi-Yi!" Faithful to her instructions she evicted me with such force and dispatch that she sent me lurching to the platform, my suitcases toppling after me.

The driver sent to meet me from Ho-Ping had no difficulty with identification. He bowed, said something unintelligible, and waved me toward a waiting van. For the next half-hour we drove into the country. It was noticeably warmer than it had been in Taipei but the air was less dense and the sky was considerably bluer. On both sides of the road rice fields stretched into the distance. They were of that special green which signalizes new life, fresh and bright, untouched by anything but rain and sunshine. Occasionally cranes whirled up out of the greenness, awkwardly stretched themselves into flying position and then took off as graceful and whimsical as kites.

From time to time as we drove further into the country I could see stone walls flanking an arched gateway leading into a courtyard and a low stone house. Here then were the houses of China, the real houses of China as I had pictured them with their slanting roofs, their graceful curves, their mythical animals precariously poised at the corners to ward off evil spirits. A far cry from the concrete bunkers of the city. My spirits rose at the sight and as we drove through the archway of Ho-Ping and I saw the spacious buildings with their classical Chinese design opening out before me, I felt comforted. Perhaps, after all, I could live here and be at peace.

The main building at Ho-Ping was my Chinese dream come true. On both sides of the round entrance door (symbol of perfection, I later learned) stretched three tiers of open stone galleries. Each was decorated with a series of evenly spaced sculptures, stone ovals, intricately incised and shaped almost like jars. The roof was slanted and the eaves were curved, just as I had imagined. And at each corner was a group of mythological animals keeping watch against evil spirits.

"Is Ho-Ping named after somebody famous?" I had asked Vincent.

CHAPTER II

"More romantic than that. It means 'Harmony'. An ideal name for a school, you must admit. It certainly beats P.S. 68."

As the van pulled up in front of the door, a young woman descended the steps. It was, I thought, a miracle that she made it safely for she had on the highest heels I had ever seen. And about her, billowing out from her miniature waist, was a skirt of pastel gossamer.

"Welcome! How are you? I am Miss Chen, secretary to President Liang. He wait for you," and she turned, motioning me to follow her up the stairs. As we started there was a rapid fire exchange between her and the driver and the van began to move off.

"My suitcases," I gestured.

"He take care," she assured me.

"Dr. Liang very happy you come," she said as she led me along the corridor. "I hope you have nice trip. My brother study in Kansas at university. You know Kansas?"

But before I could formulate an answer about whether I knew Kansas, we had arrived at Dr. Liang's office. Dr. Liang, like the architecture of Ho-Ping, was another part of the Chinese myth come true. He was tall, with a short thin beard and a face perfectly composed: the quintessential image of the Chinese scholar.

He rose and bowed and I caught myself just as I started to extend my hand. "It is my privilege to welcome you to Ho-Ping," he said and bowed again. "I trust that the trip has not been too tiring."

The tone was formal and I replied in kind. The trip had been most instructive, I assured him, and I was deeply honored by the opportunity to visit Taiwan and participate in its educational system. Another bow, an instruction in Chinese to Miss Chen, and then he motioned me to the chair beside his desk. "I have asked Miss Chen to notify our dean, Dr. Hwang, that you have arrived."

His accent was flawless and I wondered where he'd studied. "I have many happy memories of your country," he said, folding his hands on his desk. "I studied there for several years and then for a short period I was instructor in Chinese language at the Columbia University in New York City. I see from your papers that you are also from the City of New York."

But before I could answer there was a knock on the door. "Ah," he said, "Dr. Hwang has come to join us."

And with the coming of Dr. Hwang, Old China disappeared. Dr. Hwang had the manners of a salesman: quick, energetic, voluble. He shook my hand vigorously, expelled his breath in a little gust and settled into the chair I had recently occupied. Dr. Liang blinked, started to extend a hand as though to explain to Dr. Hwang that he had taken my seat; but in the end he did nothing.

Even before I had taken the small chair at the other side of Dr. Liang's desk, the dean had begun an oration on the excellence of the curriculum at Ho-Ping. He was a small man, compact, but made to seem heavier by his jacket which stretched tight across his shoulders. His English, peppered with American slang, was singularly free from grammar. Past and present, singulars and plurals, masculine and feminine pronouns were all intermingled in a loud and rapid exchange. Dr. Liang made a few gracious efforts to stop the flow but without success.

CHAPTER 11

"So, as I tell you," Dr. Hwang concluded, "we have good works for you."

I nodded. No other answer was possible.

"Maybe you have question?" he asked.

But from this Dr. Liang saved me. "I think Miss Spendler is very tired from her trip. Perhaps later she will have questions."

"O.K. with me," said Dr. Hwang getting to his feet. "Nice of you to come. See you around." And the door closed audibly behind him.

"Dr. Hwang doesn't often have the opportunity of speaking English," Dr. Liang explained. "I believe he lived in the city of Newark for a while as a young boy. His expressions are sometimes those he learned in his youth."

It was, I thought, a wonderfully diplomatic explanation. "He is, however, an excellent administrator," Dr. Liang continued. "The government made a wise choice in placing him at Ho-Ping. He has improved our rating very much. I only hope he didn't tire you too much."

I assured him that my only concern was that I hadn't followed all the intricacies of courses and scheduling that Dr. Hwang had explained.

"No cause to worry," he assured me. "All of this is clearly written and I will see that you have a copy of it in the morning. Now it is important that you see your apartment and meet Miss Schaeffer, the young lady with whom you will share it."

"I only mean this to be temporary," I assured him. I was anxious that he understood that I had no wish to inconvenience its present occupant.

"As you wish; but let me assure you that Miss Schaeffer seemed delighted that you would be sharing with her. Last year she was our only Western teacher and I think it must have been quite lonely for her. Of course her Chinese is excellent so she was able to have contact with our other teachers." He paused and smiled. "But it is not the same, is it? I learned that when I was living in the City of New York."

There was a knock on the door behind me and then I heard it open. A woman's voice said something in Chinese and Dr. Liang answered her, getting to his feet. I turned, presuming it would be the elegant Miss Chen; but instead I saw a small blond girl in sneakers and a short denim skirt.

"Hello," she said in an unmistakable British accent with just a trace of something else. "I'm Anneke Schaeffer. Welcome to Ho-Ping."

That evening Anneke introduced me to some of the necessary rituals for living safely in Chi-Yi. Be sure you never drink from the tap, even when you brush your teeth. All water must be boiled. "The trick is to remember to do it in time for it to get cool. There's nothing more maddening than going to get a glass of water and finding it still warm," Anneke warned me. As for the hard, austere bed, "You'll be glad, really; you'll see. You'd simply suffocate on a Western mattress in this climate. The bamboo mat is wonderfully cool." And the mosquito net: "An absolute necessity, although it is dreary to feel enclosed like a mummy."

When I tried to explain that I'd stay only until I could

find a place of my own, she cut me off at once.

"Let's see, shall we? You won't find it easy to get a clean comfortable place close to the college. This might work out famously for us. Heaven knows we have more space than we'd have any place else."

Anneke was right. The apartment was remarkably spacious with two good-sized bedrooms, a living room, a little kitchen and a Western bathroom. The building itself was a two-story apartment connected to a wing of the student dormitory. Originally the bottom floor had been occupied by a teacher and his family but they had moved down to Kaohsiung and the decision had been made to leave it vacant in the hope that more Western teachers might be encouraged to join the Ho-Ping faculty.

That night I lay on my bamboo mat, hearing the metallic click of the tiny lizards clinging to the walls as they waited for an unwary mosquito, and trying to absorb the day. Anneke, I had learned to my surprise, was not British. "Austrian," she explained, "but I lived in India most of my life so I do sound awfully British, I know." Her father was a mining engineer and was now exploring possibilities in Mainland China.

"It's one of the reasons I'm here, improving my Chinese so that if the China business really opens up I'll be able to go in and help him." The other reason was that she had a fiancé who was working in Hong Kong. "We were just engaged this summer. At first I thought I'd move to Hong Kong to be near Kurt. My family had lived there for a while when I was in high school so it's really not a foreign city for me. But somehow it didn't seem to work. For one thing everyone spoke Cantonese and that didn't help my

Mandarin; and the schools didn't need native English speakers the way they do here. So when they offered me a second year's contract at Ho-Ping I decided to take it. I'll get to visit Hong Kong from time to time or Kurt can come here. It's an easy trip."

Suddenly I found myself playing with my ring finger and when I looked up I found Anneke looking at me curiously. Instinctively I covered my left hand as though some telltale mark might still be visible. Our conversation ended soon after that.

"You're deathly tired," Anneke said, gathering up our teacups and taking them over to the tiny kitchen. "I'm afraid you may not sleep much; the bed takes a little getting used to but at least you can stretch out."

For a while I moved restlessly, wiping the sweat from my forehead and pushing my hair up off my neck. But it was not the heat or the strange unyielding bed that kept me awake: it was Hal. Hal with his strong shoulders and confident smile, offering me a comfortable and predictable life. Once I had returned his engagement ring we had never seen each other again and I thought I had managed to put it all behind me. I thought I had started a new life, resolute and independent. Now I was beginning to realize that a new life was not so easily fashioned.

I sat up in bed as far as my mosquito net permitted and stayed sitting like that for a while, my hands clasped around my knees. The moon was very full and bright and the curved outline of the Chinese roof of the main building stood out clearly. In the distance I could hear the unfamiliar jangle of Chinese music, broken occasionally by the sharp staccato voice of the announcer.

CHAPTER 11

I did not know what the voices of China would teach me but I was ready to listen.

III

The schedule which the dean had handed me with a conventional Chinese smile would have daunted a far more experienced teacher: two sections of English reading for fifth year students; two sections of English composition for fourth year students; one class of English literature for fifth year students preparing for the university; one class in conversation. Although there were ten teachers in the English Department, I was the only native speaker. The fact that I spoke clear idiomatic English was enough to make me a star–and to make me the recipient of the heaviest schedule.

By the end of the first day I had met all my classes. Except for the conversation class there were between fifty-five and sixty students in each. Conversation class was "very small"–only thirty-eight! The ritual with which each class began fascinated me. My students filed in in military drill and took their seats in perfect silence. I marched in after them and, as Anneke had instructed me, ascended the podium and stood at attention, while the "Class Leader" (a paragon of a drill sergeant) barked her orders: "Stand up! Bow! Sit down!"

By the end of the day the climate, the size of my classes, and the number of teaching hours left me hopelessly exhausted and when Anneke knocked at my door at six o'clock that evening I was fast asleep.

"Let's go out and eat dumplings," she suggested.

"I'm too tired, Anneke; I don't care if I eat."

"Yes, you do. Anyhow, it's not far. Just down the road a bit. It will have cooled off a little by now."

The dumpling house saw a lot of us that winter. The menu was limited: dumplings (steamed or fried, filled with pork or vegetable or something in between) and noodles–also mixed with pork or vegetable or sometimes shrimp. But it was plentiful and inexpensive and, even more important, close enough to walk to. It was easy enough to fix breakfast in our apartment and we could always get a rice box at noon in the school cafeteria but supper demanded ingenuity.

Sometimes we cooked on our little one-burner stove. Anneke was more inventive than I but even so it was more trouble than it was worth. On weekends we went down into the town, at first on the lumbering, crowded bus and then as I overcame my fear, sitting precariously behind Anneke on her little motor scooter, my arms clutching her waist.

After the first week of class my confidence rose. What teacher could ask for more than the rapt and unblinking attention with which I was regarded. It was true, my students were very quiet, very hesitant when I posed a question but this, I assured myself, was simply a matter of time. But at the end of my second week as I picked up my books and started to leave the room I became aware of a stir, a restlessness, and as I reached the open gallery I realized the class leader was following me.

"You wish to ask me something?" I stopped and smiled at her.

She nodded, clearly embarrassed.

"Am I giving you too much homework?" That was the complaint I was most used to from my former experience.

She shook her head; then slowly with a careful pause between each word, she said, "We do not understand."

I smiled indulgently. "What is it you don't understand?"

Another moment of blushing silence and then, "You," she said.

What it came to was that I spoke too quickly, too softly, not pausing between words, between sentences.

And so began the exhausting regime of speaking slowly, with deliberate care, being sure that words did not run into each other and in a voice that out-matched the volume of sound that swept in from the adjacent classrooms.

"But how could they keep looking at me as though they were hanging on every sentence when they don't understand a word I'm saying?" I fumed to Anneke that evening.

"They wish to be polite."

"What's the point of sitting there as though everything is fine when they don't understand what I'm saying?"

"But from their point of view complaining like that would have seemed like admonishing you, correcting you. You might easily have been angry and offended. After all you are the teacher and the teacher is always correct. The class leader did a very courageous thing. I'm sure they discussed it for a long time before they decided to act."

The episode colored everything for me. How was I ever to know what was really happening, what they were thinking behind those obedient dark eyes? When I gave a test, their answers were letter-perfect, couched in exactly the same words I had used in class. Their memories were uncanny; not a detail escaped them. It was all stored up to repeat at the appropriate moment. Yet when I asked if they liked a story or a poem or a character they were tongue-tied, sitting before me straight and contained, all eyes lowered on their desks.

If I called on a student she stood obediently, her arms at her sides, her eyes on the floor.

"Did you like the story?" I asked.

No answer.

"Have you read the story?"

"Do you remember the names of the characters?"

She remembered them perfectly. She remembered the plot, the conflict, the resolution.

Back to Round One.

"Did you like the story?"

Again the same unwavering silence.

Only when I said, "I liked it very much. I thought it was a fine story," did the eyes come up, meeting mine. Now they were on solid ground again; knowing what I thought, they knew what they should think.

That is how I noticed Li Mei-Lan. At the end of one of my exhausting (and unsuccessful) efforts to get them to form an opinion, to think through a question on their own, I turned suddenly toward the windows and met the eyes of Li Mei-Lan. In place of the look of studied attention I had grown used to, I saw something close to a smile. It was gone in an instant. Her eyes were lowered and she slipped invisibly into the majority. I had been teaching for more than a month and this was my first moment of feeling a personal contact, an instant of reciprocal understanding. I watched Mei-Lan carefully for the rest of the week but in vain. There was not the slightest motion to distinguish her.

That weekend as I corrected compositions I kept an eye out for Mei-Lan's. The paragraph she had handed in was correctly written but had nothing to distinguish it from a dozen others until I came to the final sentence. Of the heroine of the short story we had been reading, Mei-Lan had written: "I admire Joan. I think she is a clever girl."

The sentence was startling. It expressed an opinion–her own, not one I had endorsed. The Mei-Lan who had for an instant revealed herself in class had now–and this time in the permanence of writing–revealed herself again.

I felt a thrill, an inner excitement, a sense of power wholly disproportionate to the event. But there it was. I attacked the remainder of my compositions with renewed interest. Perhaps my teaching was not so hopeless as I had thought. Perhaps there was the possibility of bringing my students–at least some of them–to a new level of thought where they would be more than parrots. Perhaps I would see that secret smile in Mei-Lan's eyes again. Perhaps I could tutor her on the side, perhaps we could read some books together. Perhaps she could get a scholarship to an American university–some fine school, not one of the little fifth rate colleges where the Taiwanese were generally accepted. And by then I would be back in New York, able to help her . . . . And when she graduated . . . .

With that first inner surge of pleasure my Great Dream for Li Mei-Lan had begun to form.

CHAPTER III

That night as Anneke and I were having supper–our inevitable Saturday night feast of shrimp and noodles–I asked her, "Do you remember teaching a Li Mei-Lan last year?"

"Ummmm, I don't think so. What does she look like?"

We both giggled. It was our secret ethnic joke–a variation on "All Orientals look alike." But, in fact, with their identical coloring, their identical uniforms, their identical hair cuts, prescribed by national standards, "What does she look like?" was a useless question.

"Is she giving you trouble?" Anneke asked. "Not that I can imagine such a thing."

"On the contrary, she's giving me joy. I just read her composition. She actually expressed an opinion of her own."

When Anneke said nothing, I urged, "Aren't you impressed?"

"I don't know. Why are you impressed?"

"Because I've been trying so hard to make them understand that it's not enough just to parrot everything I say, that to be really educated you must be able to form opinions of your own, not just say what you think will please the teacher."

Anneke laughed. "But this girl has done just that."

"Just what?"

"Just pleased the teacher. She knows you want an opinion so she has given you an opinion. That's no different from the others, only a little bit sharper."

Anneke's judgment irked me. It made me feel stupid. For the next few weeks I kept a careful watch on Mei-Lan. Her work was good but not extraordinary; her behavior in class was undistinguished. I could observe nothing that would separate her from her classmates. Perhaps there was nothing, I was beginning to think. Perhaps wishful thinking had made me read something that was not there.

I was beginning to settle in with my students now and they with me. I discovered that they loved to work in groups and that if they were bolstered by their peers it became possible for them to form quite definite opinions. One day when we had finished reading a short story in which a man was severely punished for disobeying the law, even though his reason for doing so was to save the life of a friend, I decided to provide maximum class participation. I set up a full courtroom scene with prosecutor, defender and jury. It was an ambitious project and it took me an entire period to set up the guidelines, explain the process and the roles each would play. They would have time, I explained, to meet in groups, to discuss the aspects of the case and then on the appointed day we would all come to court.

I preened myself on the project. It seemed to me ideal. It would give them a chance to practice their English in a more exciting session, it would force them to arrive at some opinion, and it would give them a chance to act–something, I discovered, which despite their apparent shyness they loved to do. The jury, I explained, had three possible verdicts available: the man could be found guilty of the crime, found innocent of the crime, or found guilty but with extenuating circumstances.

CHAPTER III

On the day of the trial the classroom was filled with excitement. The desks had been shifted to make room for a jury box and a witness stand. When the bell rang for the beginning of class the simulated courtroom was in perfect order. I sat in the back, eager to watch the success of my experiment. The prosecutor and her assistants surprised me with their verbal skill–and their vehemence. The defense was pitifully weak, almost apologetic in its arguments. When the case went to the jury the verdict was quick and unanimous: the prisoner was guilty.

Now was the time I had set aside for comments, questions, objections from the class. To my surprise not a single hand was raised. Even the condemned sat motionless, head bowed in apparent consent. I waited for a few minutes and then I asked if anyone would like to ask a question. Silence. Would anyone like to speak in favor of the prisoner or argue against the verdict? As I looked around at the bowed heads I realized I was asking too much. To run so counter to public opinion was asking the impossible.

I stood and walked to the front of the room, resuming my position of authority. "I would like to speak against the verdict," I said, hoping my voice would inspire them with courage. After all, what the teacher said was generally regarded as the last word. "I would like to ask the jury to show mercy to this man. Although he broke the law, he did it for a greater good. Had he not broken the law his friend would have died. So, although he is guilty, he is guilty with extenuating circumstances."

I expected my opinion to find immediate support but this time there was no responsive nod. They sat, looking straight ahead, their hands folded in their laps, their feet firm on the floor. The opposition was palpable. The court of law which I had set up had turned upon me. The imaginary situation had become real. I was the defendant and I had been condemned. Something had happened for which I had had no rehearsal. I stood alone, surrounded by immense space. The students' desks had been pushed to the side and the teacher's desk and podium were at the far corner of the room. There was nothing for me to hold onto but the witness chair. I looked up but there were no responsive eyes. Instead I gazed into the large portrait hanging on the back wall: Chiang Kai-Shek, in full military regalia, looked back at me, his face strong and unlined, and on his lips a slight smile of unutterable contempt.

I should, of course, have left it there; but like any defendant I needed to show that I had done nothing wrong, that the opinion I had expressed had validity. Thus I did what I should never have done: I pleaded my case, innocently, unaware of the full import of what I was saying. In some foolish, guileless American way I began to talk about innocence and guilt, about just laws and unjust laws, about legalism and how it undermines the human spirit. And then I flung myself straight into disaster: there is an obligation, I argued, to change unjust laws and sometimes the only way to change them is by disobeying them, by refusing to comply with them.

For a moment there was silence and then the prosecutor stood, strengthened by the backing of her classmates–and her country. She brushed aside my arguments with a simple statement: "He is guilty. It is the law."

At that moment I turned away, humiliated, and my eyes met Mei-Lan's. She was looking straight at me and in those dark eyes was the light of an intelligence I had never seen before, a kind of knowledge beyond my understanding. It was neither sympathy nor condemnation. Mei-Lan had a keen apprehension of all that was happening in that classroom, a knowledge that so far eluded me. Our gaze held for a moment and then she looked down.

I was in very fact saved by the bell. With the first whirr I was released from whatever spell had bound us all. At once and as always books were piled neatly at the side of the desks, the class leader barked out her drill-sergeant order and the class rose to its feet. They bowed, they chorused, "Thank you, Miss Spendler," and they marched in impeccable order out the door. Mei-Lan marched with them in unbroken rhythm.

My face was flaming; I could feel it. My next class was in seven minutes–a younger group–and together we prepared an outline for a composition on "The city I would most like to visit." I made no effort to encourage class participation. I was glad to sit at my desk and oversee their dark heads intent on their task. Class followed class leaving me no time to reflect. But I could feel the hot flush diminish and by afternoon the sharp pain–a mixture of emotions I could hardly name–had eased off.

But even when the teaching day was over, one more task remained: my weekly calligraphy lesson. Had I had another teacher I might have begged off for the day–but not with Madame Hsu. Madame Hsu was not native Taiwanese. Like so many she had come to the Island from the Mainland at the time of the Communist takeover. When we first began our lessons I was eager to know something of her history but she rebuffed my questions with a harshness that was almost brutal. She must once have been a beautiful woman, I thought; it was still evident in the delicate disciplined mouth and the fine-boned features of the northern Chinese. But now she seemed almost like a caricature of the implacable Chinese woman. The lines about her nose were deep and hard and her mouth was pulled down into an arc that paralleled her eyebrows.

At our first meeting I tried to tell her something about myself, of my interest in art, of my happiness in having the opportunity to study Chinese calligraphy; but she brushed all this aside without response. She made sharing something of our lives, our interests, seem superficial, almost childish. Since then all my efforts to smile, to show my admiration for her own stunning calligraphy had been repulsed. Even so, I could ask for no finer teacher. Madame Hsu was not only an expert in technique but she had the ability to explain and guide.

Although there were never any words of praise for my efforts, a single gratified nod was enough to exhilarate me. But today I knew I would never be able to discipline myself to Madame Hsu's rigorous standard. Usually we began by examining the brush strokes I had practiced for homework but today she pushed them aside and set me a new task. I took my brush and tried to emulate the fluid stroke she executed so easily but my hand was too tense and instead of the single long stroke the character demanded, I hesitated midway and produced two wobbly lines. She pushed the paper aside.

"Again," she said.

And again I dipped my brush in the ink and positioned my arm. Even before I had finished the stroke she had pulled the paper away from me.

"Put down the brush. Now pick it up and hold it as you have been taught."

CHAPTER III

I tried again but my fingers were shaking as I tried to fix them correctly against the smooth circle of the brush.

She wrenched it from my hand with an expression of contempt. "Where is your discipline? You cannot write when you are so out of harmony. Your brush will reveal your soul."

Tears were stinging my eyes but I dared not raise my hand to brush them away. It would be too humiliating.

"Even now," she continued, "with so much practice, you hold your brush as though it were a Western paintbrush. Writing is not painting. A child just beginning school makes a better stroke."

I blinked to keep the tears back but instead one fell on the still wet ink of my last effort. The ink spread slowly, radiating into a misshapen circle, distorting even further my awkward downward stroke. The blurred image released my tears. I no longer cared that I was crying; I no longer feared Madame Hsu's humiliations. Perhaps now she would understand how harsh, how cruel, she was being to me. Self-pity inundated me. Perhaps she would realize how hard it was to be in a foreign country, to be alone, to be . . . . I reached for a handkerchief and wiped my eyes.

"I'm sorry," I said righteously, "I've had a very difficult day at school."

But there was no response to my plea for sympathy. Instead Madame Hsu removed the top sheet of paper and placed a clean one in its place.

"The stroke that we are executing this afternoon is a very beautiful one but it must be made with great control, with a swift but disciplined motion."

She held my brush out to me and I took it.

"Again," she said.

My hand was still shaking and I jabbed unsteadily at the paper. She said nothing and I struggled across the lined page, angry and humiliated at my own ineptness.

She took another piece of paper and held it before me. "You will try again but this time larger. Steady and quick, a single stroke."

I had reached up to dry my tears and when I took up my brush again my fingers were wet.

"Please, take your handkerchief and dry your fingers. You will have no control over your brush unless your hand is cool and dry."

It was the only allusion she made to my tears. For exactly fifty minutes we continued my lesson.

"Now," she said, as she looked at her watch, "for next week you will practice the entire character like this," and she executed two more exquisite strokes to complete the character. "And if you have time you should go to a small exhibit at the Buddhist Temple. One of the monks there is a fine master. His work will help you to see what you are striving for."

For the first time that day she looked straight at me, a look hard and uncompromising. "Do you understand?"

"Yes," I said, "I understand." Strangely enough I found myself able to return her look without resentment.

CHAPTER III

I walked back to our apartment too tired to think. I lay on my bed and watched the two small lizards (Alphonse and Alphonsine, Anneke had named them) perform their acrobatics on our ceiling. Since that terrible morning class I had looked forward to this hour when I would have time to think, time to figure it out, time to cry in sheer shame and frustration. But now I lay quite still. In some totally unexpected way Madame Hsu had strengthened me. She had, almost brutally, refused my cry for help, my plea for sympathy. She had forced me on. She had willed strength for me and in the end that long unrelenting look had been her commendation.

After a while I got up and fixed some rice and cabbage and made a cup of instant coffee and took it out to our little balcony, overlooking the school grounds. The students who lived in the dormitory–about two hundred of them–were already at their studies and there was no one on the grounds except the old workman who lived in a dilapidated shack by the gate. Now he sat under a tree playing with three little puppies born to his pet dog just a month ago.

I sat and watched the moon come up. Although it was December I needed only a thin sweater. It was Anneke's night for her Chinese language class which kept her out until ten and although I was anxious to tell her about what had happened that morning, I found I was too tired to wait up any longer. It would have to wait until the next evening. Maybe it would be better that way. By then I might have a more objective reading. Maybe by morning I'd see that my reaction was exaggerated. Anneke would probably shrug her shoulders and tell me to brush the whole episode aside, that nothing good would come of rehearsing it. Yet that old passion to make things right, to talk them out and come to agreement was too strong to ignore. Long after I had gone to bed, I kept reliving my morning class hoping to find some way to create a positive ending. Perhaps I should set aside a period to go back over the episode, explaining what I had hoped to accomplish and why I was disappointed at their response. I fell asleep rehearsing what I would say.

But in the morning I knew I wouldn't do it. I simply didn't know how. Twenty-four hours ago I would have said that I had begun to understand my students, that we had achieved a certain rapprochement. Now I approached them not only as an alien but as an alien in enemy territory. The desire to confront and explain was gone; I simply wanted to avoid controversy at all costs. I flipped through the table of contents in the short story book and suddenly even these familiar domestic tales seemed full of perils. I pushed them aside and took up our small anthology of poetry. My students were romantics in many ways. They loved nature, loved to dream of escaping their crowded noisy city into the peace of the countryside. I would save myself in the poetry of Robert Frost. I would talk to them about New England in the winter, about the soft drift of snow against pine trees, of country roads and little villages where a white church steeple rose clean against a blue sky. I would make it all quite wonderful and new and untouched. Somehow I would regain my ascendency.

I was only fifteen minutes into my introduction when a young woman who worked in the president's office beckoned me from the door.

"Colonel Sheng wish to see you," she said in slowly articulated English.

CHAPTER III

I looked at my watch. "Tell him I have class until a quarter past eleven. I'll come then."

My reply was clearly unexpected and unacceptable. She shook her head. "He see you now," she said.

"Tell him I'm in class now. I'll come as soon as I'm free," I answered and walked back into the classroom.

For a moment she stood at the door watching me and then she walked back down the hall.

Short as the interruption had been it had ruptured the tone I had been trying to establish. It was clear that my students were far more curious about what had happened in the hall than about "the path not taken."

I hardly had time to reintroduce my subject before the same messenger appeared again. This time she entered without knocking, walking straight to my desk. Despite the high heels, the full graceful skirt, the delicate porcelain features, she had the bearing of a soldier under orders.

"Please, you come with me," she said and waited for me to precede her out the door.

"Just a minute," I said; "please wait outside." Whether she understood or not, I don't know, but she never moved from my side. Clearly she had received her orders and would obey them.

Slowly, so as not to lose more face, I gave my students an assignment, pointed out the page with the poem I wanted them to read and the list of study questions they were to reflect on, assuring them that I would be back before the end of the period.

I had never met Colonel Sheng, although I had often

seen him wandering about, sometimes dressed in military uniform, sometimes in civilian clothes. He was a small man with a badly pock-marked face and thick, black-rimmed glasses.

"Who is he?" I asked Anneke one day. "He gives me the creeps."

"He's the security man," she explained.

Clearly he fit no image I had of a security guard.

Anneke shook her head. "Not a guard," she said. "A government man–more like your CIA. His job is to protect internal security, to see that there are no infiltrators, no spies."

"Here at Ho-Ping!" The idea seemed ludicrous.

It was Colonel Sheng, Anneke explained, who had the government responsibility for resident aliens at Ho-Ping. It was he who had checked my passport, my residence permit, my university transcripts. Now he waited for me in his office, an impressive office, far bigger than that of the president or the dean.

Today he was in full military uniform. There was a chair at the side of his desk but he did not ask me to sit. I stood before him, while he continued to examine papers on his desk. On the wall behind him hung the same supercilious image of Chiang Kai-Shek which hung in every classroom. The portrait, however, was much larger and bordered by a heavy gilt frame.

"You are Miss Leslie Spendler?" His "l"s were terrible, making my name almost unintelligible.

"Yes," I answered.

CHAPTER III

"I think you teach literature to fourth and fifth year students?"

"That is correct." What had happened to my self-confidence that even simple questions seemed like traps set to ensnare me, traps I was too awkward to evade?

He shifted in his chair and I saw the holster with his gun hanging from his belt. "What do you teach?" he asked, suddenly looking up at me.

The question took me off-guard. My mind had been racing ahead, expecting to be asked about my college activities, what organizations I had been a member of, what magazines I subscribed to–all those questions the movies had taught me were the standard fare addressed to political detainees.

"I teach English and American literature."

"What kind of literature?"

"Well, I teach some poetry, some plays, short stories, a novel."

"What does a teacher include in this study?"

Now I was hopelessly adrift, unable to find the line that might protect me. "What will help the students understand the literature–characterization, use of language . . . . "

"Does it also include political opinions?" The question was fired at me as though he had drawn his gun.

I looked down in silence. At that moment I could think of nothing that would not entrap me further.

"We have permitted you into our country in good

faith," Colonel Sheng continued, looking down at his desk. He had in front of him copies of all the documents relative to my residence permit. "We have accepted your statements about yourself and your occupation without question. Perhaps in America where anything is permitted you can speak and act as you wish. In this country we have standards. We believe in our government and are loyal to it. We will not permit it to be undermined by aliens."

I was filled with a fear I had never before experienced. It was different from the fear of walking down a dark deserted street, different from the fear of losing someone dear to you. It was a fear that sprang from the realization of being totally alone. There was nothing in that room or in that school that I could count on to be my advocate. Yet despite my terror his contemptuous reference to the United States angered me and I found my voice.

"I have never said or done anything contrary to your standards," I answered. "Why would I?"

He shrugged. "How do we know why you have come here or with what goals in mind?"

"My only goal has been to improve the English of my students." I could hear the tremor in my voice but at least I was speaking.

"You did not advocate the overthrow of laws that interfere with personal interest?"

"Certainly not."

But it was clear my answer was not good enough. He was on to something I had said the day before and he intended to go on worrying it. Desperately I tried to recall exactly what I had said during those few impassioned moments when I had pleaded for mercy in a chauvinistic burst against legalism and misguided justice.

"Do you deny that these are your words?" asked Colonel Sheng, opening a notebook and turning the leaves until he found two pages clipped together. And then he read, word for word, my foolish speech about just and unjust laws, our obligation to disobey what is unjust, my endorsement of civil disobedience. Taken out of context and articulated in Colonel Sheng's slow, faulty English the words were devastating.

I shook my head impatiently, determined to make him understand the situation in which I had spoken. "You see, it was just a game we were playing. We weren't talking about Taiwan. We were simply looking at a fictional character, at a story."

He hardly listened to me. "Are these your words? You spoke these words yesterday in a classroom with fifty-eight students?"

Then, suddenly, the means by which those words had reached him with such devastating accuracy, burst upon me. One of those poised, intelligent young students who honored me with their unflagging attention, who bowed and smiled and thanked me for being their teacher, one of them had listened sentence by sentence and then used her impeccable memory to betray me.

The realization put me beyond fear and the remainder of Colonel Sheng's harangue hardly touched me.

"I warn you," he was saying, "we cannot have foreigners expressing dangerous political opinions. If you continue to preach these things then . . . ." He made a gesture of tearing a paper in half. "Then your permission to live here in Taiwan will be revoked. You understand?"

I nodded. There was no point in explanation. He made no gesture of dismissal but simply turned to busy himself with other papers on his desk.

When I got to the hall the bell for the end of class was ringing. I walked up the back stairs, the ones the students didn't use, and entered my classroom through the south entrance. The room was empty and in perfect order except for my desk. Two books on Robert Frost lay open and next to them the outline I had made for my morning class. On the side of the desk were some pictures I had clipped from a magazine–New England in the fall: brilliant and clean and free.

IV

"Don't be so upset," Anneke tried to console me when, finally, we had time to talk about my encounter with Colonel Sheng. "That one just likes to talk loud; you know how the military are. Nothing bad will happen."

I shook my head. My initial fear had been replaced by righteous anger. "That's not the point, whether anything bad happens; it's deeper than that. The whole business is so appalling."

"Appalling that something you said in your classroom should be so blown out of proportion?"

"Partially that. Appalling that I'm not free to express an opinion without having it reported as though I were in some penal institution."

Anneke shrugged. "Americans have very limited political imaginations. Perhaps it's a weakness that comes from living in a democracy."

Her response irritated me. It was almost as though she were out of sympathy with me.

"Aren't you appalled," I asked, "that some off-the-cuff opinion I expressed in a classroom should be taken up by a government official? And what's even worse that one of my students should go behind my back and report me? It's so sneaky!"

"From your point of view. From hers it may be a duty of loyalty to her country."

"To spy on her teacher?"

"But what you did was quite public. She had no need to spy, as you call it. Perhaps you are not aware that in each class there is a member of the Youth Corps whose duty it is to observe and inform, to report any incident, any discussion by either the teacher or the students which might be considered deviant."

I hardly grasped the import of what she was telling me. "But what I was saying was so obvious, so routine–why would such a thing seem so important?"

"Because it was, in fact, quite a deviation from what they are taught. Because you are an American, a nice American, it's true, but a Westerner all the same and they have been taught to beware of the West as a source of immorality and dangerous liberalism. Don't forget, Leslie," she warned, "your students have been taught all their lives that they live in the most perfect country in the world. Since they have no experience to contradict this, it doesn't occur to them to question it."

But this I couldn't swallow. "You can't make me believe that all those intelligent young women who are more alert and more industrious than most American students believe everything they're told without questioning."

Again Anneke shrugged. "Perhaps not, but if they have doubts they keep them to themselves."

"So you're not appalled that someone in my class went and reported verbatim–really verbatim–what I had said?"

"It would be more comfortable if these things didn't happen, but I'm not appalled."

CHAPTER IV

"The worst of it is that I have no idea who is responsible. Every day I'll keep watching them, wondering which one it is."

"Leslie, give it up. It won't do you any good, I assure you. You will never find out, no matter how hard you try. Yes, someone did it. Perhaps more than one. Perhaps out of loyalty to her country, perhaps to gain merit with the Youth Corps, perhaps to curry favor with Colonel Sheng. Who knows? But don't try to find out. You will never succeed and it will color everything you do with suspicion."

I knew she was right but I wondered how I could ever again face those sharp intelligent faces without suspicion and resentment.

"Will the rest of the class know what happened?" I asked.

"Clearly they know that Colonel Sheng sent for you and it won't be hard for them to guess for what. Will they know who reported you? Probably not. That's the great Chinese mystery: a society that is so closely knit and yet with individuals who are so secret. Be grateful, Leslie, that today is Saturday and that you won't have to meet that class again until Monday."

The next day Anneke persuaded me to go into Chi-Yi with her. "You need to get away. Come on, we'll ride down and wander about the market."

Sundays were precious, the only completely free day in our week. Some of our classes met on Saturday mornings and Saturday afternoons were very often taken up with school functions and extra tutoring. Fortunately I had conquered my fear of motorcycles sufficiently to ride behind Anneke on her little Honda–although I was still subject to moments of fright. The four-lane highways were never empty. Huge trucks roared by, honking continuously, their top-heavy loads listing dangerously. On both sides of us other motorcycles scooted by, rarely with fewer than three people and sometimes with as many as five: father, mother, two small children and a baby clutched in the mother's arms or hanging from her neck.

The slowest moving vehicles were the bicycles but these had their own dangers as crates of ducks and chickens balanced precariously behind the driver. Speed was apparently the first concern–safety the last. The talent for acrobatics was clearly in the genes and I watched in awe as vehicles slid in and out with only inches to spare and then righted themselves just at the crucial moment.

The volume of traffic and the accent on speed took their toll in accidents, sometimes very bad ones. We were about half-way into the city when an old gentleman just in front of us with a crate of live chickens roped on the back of his bicycle was forced to the side of the road by a motorcycle. Anneke swerved just in time to miss him and I looked back to see if he was all right. He had lost his balance, and fallen over on top of his bicycle. The crash had broken the crate and released the chickens. The old man himself lay there, the chickens with their bound feet flapping and squawking about him, while the traffic rolled on.

"No one is stopping," I yelled at Anneke; but she shook her head, unable to hear me through the traffic. I tried again but unsuccessfully.

When we got into the city and parked the Honda, Anneke took off her helmet and shook out her hair.

CHAPTER IV

"What were you trying to say to me back there?"

"That old man with the chickens that we passed, he was knocked off his bicycle and nobody stopped to help him."

"They're probably afraid."

"Afraid? Afraid of what?"

"That they'll be held responsible for the accident and have to pay the damages."

"That's inhuman." That old thin body with its wispy beard had become my cause.

"But human, too, from the other person's point of view."

"And it doesn't bother you, you think it's 'human' to leave an old man on the side of the road where he could be killed if he isn't already dead?"

"Of course it bothers me but it doesn't shock me quite the way it shocks you. Remember, I've lived in India and Hong Kong and Argentina. The world isn't all full of nice people who stop to pick people up on the street. I don't like it but I know I can't change it. Come on, Les, your old fellow is probably back on his bicycle with his chickens and riding home by now. They're a tough race, you know."

But even the "Golden Emperor's Garden Tea House" with its dragon-leaf tea and little bean cakes could not change my mood.

"How about a wander through the market?" Anneke suggested.

But I shook my head. "Let's go home." All my old fears had returned and the thought of the trip back terrified me. We rode home with my arms locked around Anneke's waist, my teeth clamped tight, as the traffic swirled around us. As we passed the scene of the accident I tried to see around the sides of the trucks to the other side of the road but there seemed to be no sign of the old man and his chickens. Perhaps Anneke was right; perhaps he was home, safe with his chickens. Perhaps I was the foolish one after all.

Whatever harrowing expectations I had built up about my Monday class were for naught.

"You'll see," Anneke assured me as we drank our morning coffee. "There will not be a shade of difference. Everything will be absolutely normal. You wait and see."

"Except for me."

"No, you too. No matter how you feel you cannot show it. If you lose face now it will change your whole year here."

"I've already lost face."

"No, you haven't." Anneke was adamant. "Nobody really knows what happened with Colonel Sheng."

"Except for one person."

"And she will never reveal herself. So it is all up to you. Smile and teach your class as you always do. You'll see. It will all work out."

She was right, of course. There was not a nuance of expression or gesture that was out of the ordinary. Once or twice I looked toward Mei-Lan but she never met my gaze. As for the others, they were their usual polite, industrious selves.

As Anneke had predicted, nothing was appreciably changed by my encounter with Colonel Sheng. I helped my students to interpret English literature, to increase their vocabulary and to express themselves idiomatically. I had no difficulty in fulfilling my responsibilities. I had no strong bent toward political comment and as a teacher I was far more concerned with improving their English than in stirring their political consciences. For all practical purposes my life was left unchanged. Yet something had changed. The change was in me. Something soft and pliable had been sharpened. I felt like a woman who has been mugged in broad daylight and on a pleasant street. An uneasiness had been bred in me and I knew I would never walk carefree in the same way again.

Yet despite this I had begun to settle in with my students. By the end of November the myth of the quiet, impassive, inscrutable Oriental had been exploded, for I discovered that (except for the discipline of the classroom) my students were gregarious, noisy and full of an ironic and earthy humor which both jolted and delighted me. I was also learning with Anneke's help to scale down their hyperboles. "You are a golden teacher" or "Your lessons are like spring rain to my mind" could, I discovered, be translated into American as "You're OK". Conversely, I learned to brush aside their own humble protestations. Statements like : "I am a very stupid girl" or "I am the ugly one in my family" I soon learned had nothing to do with a poor self-image but were the stock-in-trade of Chinese etiquette. Ambition far exceeded humility as I discovered as we prepared for the National Speech Contest.

"It is the biggest event of the year," Anneke explained.

"It can change their lives."

"Yes," she affirmed when I looked sceptical. "If a student places high in this it will guarantee her a place in the National University. Otherwise," she shrugged, "maybe she stays a secretary all her life."

"If it's so important, they shouldn't have asked me to be the coach. I don't know a thing about speech contests."

Anneke shook her head impatiently. "That's not the point. The point is you speak English. You have to do it, Leslie. They would never understand if you refused; they would think you didn't want Ho-Ping to do well."

And so I began the onerous task of preparing for the National Speech Contest. Even though only four out of the four hundred fifth-year students could place in the finals, the initial winnowing was easy. The stars shone very bright. As we reached the quarter finals the choices became increasingly thorny and painful. Underneath the gracious smiles and deprecating bows, the students were fighting for their lives–and everyone knew it.

By the week before the contest I had narrowed the field to eight contestants. The semi-finals were held in the school auditorium on a damp grey December afternoon. For the next two hours I listened to their prepared speeches ("The Meaning of Moon Feast," "The Origin of Chinese Opera," "The Excellence of the Palace Museum") and then to the one minute extempore speeches whose topics were assigned on the spot.

I listened, observed, corrected, took notes, concentrating on any detail that would help me to distinguish the four best. When we had finished I thanked them, congratulated them on superior performances and told them that the four finalists would be announced the following day at the beginning of Assembly. Then I gathered up my papers and walked home alone.

I mulled over my notes while Anneke was getting dinner. It was fairly easy to winnow out the three poorest and fairly easy, too, to pick the two best. But this left three students vying for the two coveted remaining places: Fong Li-Hwa, the class leader; Chiang Yu-Be, the student with the highest general average; and Li Mei-Lan.

"Come and have dinner," Anneke called. "We can talk about it together."

As I stood up, pushing aside a folder with a set of quizzes I had brought home to correct, a small piece of paper slipped to the floor. On it, printed very clearly, was written: The girl is Fong Li-Hwa.

The extraordinary thing, it seems to me now, is that I had not a moment's hesitation in interpreting the message. It was immediately clear: I was being informed that it was Fong Li-Hwa who had reported me to Colonel Sheng. I walked to the doorway, the paper in my hands.

"Whatever is it?" Anneke asked. "You look as though you'd been struck dumb."

"Read it," I said, handing her the paper.

She read it, scowling, and then looked up at me. "What is it?"

"It's the name of the girl who informed on me."

"Are you sure?"

"Perfectly sure."

"Where did you find it?"

"It fell out of my folder, the one I keep test papers in."

"When did you notice it?"

"Just now. When I stood up."

"But it could be anything," Anneke was floundering. "It's just a name, after all. How can you be so sure?"

I had no explanation but my certitude was absolute. I knew.

"Who could have put it there?" Anneke asked.

"Anyone. I always leave the folder on my desk so that if someone is handing in a late paper she can just slip it in."

"But why now? It's weeks since Colonel Sheng sent for you."

For a moment I had no answer but suddenly it was very clear: the Speech Contest. That little slip of paper was not simply to curry favor with me but to ensure the elimination of a rival. In that light it all made a terrible kind of sense.

Anneke nodded when I explained. "Possible," she said. "Ambition is a powerful goad. Let me see it again," Anneke asked, reaching across the table. "Who is Fong Li-Hwa?"

"One of the final contestants in the speech contest. It is between her and Mei-Lan. I hadn't made up my mind yet."

Suddenly panic struck. "What am I going to do?" I asked. "I feel trapped."

"Well in a way you are. It is what the writer hopes for, that this note will corrupt your judgment. And you can't let that happen. First of all, destroy that note. Tear it into pieces and burn it with the candle."

She picked up the note and put it in my hand. "Don't wait; do it now," she said. "Banish it. It has no place in your decisions. Give yourself two more hours to review their work and then make your judgment. Write down the names of the finalists. Whatever you write is irrevocable. If it helps you can give it to me until you make the announcement tomorrow. Are you with me?" Anneke was implacable.

That night before we went to bed I gave Anneke the names of the finalists. The contended fourth place had gone to Li Mei-Lan.

I lay for a while looking up at the ceiling through the design of my mosquito net and wondering about fairness. Although I had agreed to Anneke's proposal, the truth was that that small piece of paper still had power over me. My eyes ached with fatigue but when I closed them I saw again that carefully printed name and I could not sleep. Nor could I banish the images of those students who might have been responsible. Once so indistinguishable to me, now they were clearly distinguished.

And of them all it was Li Mei-Lan who was etched most sharply. Of them all I had sensed in Mei-Lan a curious intelligence, a perception cool and hard. That she was ambitious I had no doubt. "Your star," Anneke laughingly called her when I came home praising her performance. But now the simple pleasure I had found in fostering Mei-Lan's ability was tainted with distrust. I could not dispel the suspicion that it was Mei-Lan who had slipped that piece of paper into my folder.

I was too restless to stay in bed and I got up and poured a glass of water from my thermos. It was tepid, as usual, and it seemed to me that I could taste the sediment on my tongue. I stood looking out the window. There was just enough moon to outline the main building with its classical round door, symbolizing perfection. I had once thought it was the most beautiful piece of architecture on campus but now that, too, was tainted by my distrust.

What was happening to me? How could I have become so obsessed by the action of some ambitious girl, barely out of her teens, whose identity I would probably never know? It was all so small, so insignificant–like the Island. Even Colonel Sheng with his military bravado, who was he really? Some third rate officer in the service of a country without stature or power. And yet I was becoming a captive, a prisoner, subtly subjected to that peculiar Chinese policy of "reeducation". My world was tilting; all my firm moral verticals were at an angle. I was losing my balance.

That afternoon the names of the four finalists were posted on the official bulletin board. In my final class I called the name of each one and congratulated her. Each stood, received the applause of her classmates and made some humble statement, acknowledging that she was a very poor speaker who did not deserve this honor but that she would do her best for the honor of her college. If I had expected the slightest indication of anything beyond humble acknowledgement I was disappointed. Even my overt glance at Mei-Lan showed me nothing more than an earnest school girl, modest and contained.

CHAPTER IV

That afternoon when I came home there were two large packages on the kitchen table–one from Germany for Anneke and the other from my parents. Both were securely tied with the tell-tale yellow tape that indicated they had been carefully scrutinized by customs before being delivered to us.

"In case you have forgotten," Anneke said, cutting the tape on her package, "next Friday is Christmas and we are going to celebrate."

"How? We only have one day."

"Then we will have a one-day celebration. Whatever we decide on I'm going to get you out of here for a day. No argument. How about going down to Kan-Ting? I've never been but it's right on the ocean and there's a bus we can get from Chi-Yi. We'll go early, maybe we can even get a swim–it's still warm enough–have a real Chinese feast and get back here early in the evening."

But Anneke's Christmas celebration never came off. Four days before Christmas our lives changed dramatically. I had just come in from class when the phone rang. I hated to answer the phone; I was never able to understand even the most obvious formulas. This call was worse than most. I thought the operator said "Hong Kong" but before I could hear any more there was an insistent crackling, a loud click, and the phone went dead. Our phone was connected to the main switchboard of the college but I knew it was worse than useless to contact them. Anyway, I reasoned, if it were from Hong Kong it was probably for Anneke. Kurt often called although he generally waited until evening.

"There was a phone call a little while ago," I told her when she came in about an hour later. "I think it was from

Hong Kong."

She frowned. "Kurt never calls so early."

"Maybe he was calling to tell you he got some extra time off." Anneke had been disappointed that Kurt could not come to spend Christmas with her. I heard the phone ring again when I was in taking my shower and when I came out Anneke was standing motionless in the doorway.

"It was from a hospital in Hong Kong. Kurt's been in a motorcycle accident."

"Is he . . . ?" I hardly knew how to say it.

"He's OK, they said. He's not critical but he has many injuries. They said he was conscious but I couldn't speak with him." She stood for a minute rubbing her hand over the cradle of the phone. "I'm going to go. There's a plane around nine. I need to borrow money, Les."

I took what I had out of my wallet and out of the box I kept locked in my desk drawer. "It's not very much," I said, handing it to her.

"It's all right; I don't need very much, just enough to get my ticket. Once I get to Hong Kong I'll be all right. We have friends there and the people at Kurt's office will help. They know my family."

She was surprisingly cool as we drove to the airport. She had written a note of explanation to the president and the dean and in the taxi she gave me further instructions about her classes, her syllabus, her quarterly grades.

"Don't wait," she said, as she checked her bag. "I'll be fine. I'll call you tomorrow night and tell you how things are," she said as the Hong Kong flight began to board.

CHAPTER IV

It was dark when I went out to find a taxi to take me back to Ho-Ping but even so the traffic had not diminished. We cut and swerved between lorries and motor scooters, honking our way ahead of bicycles and narrowly missing pedestrians trying to cross the highway. The guard at Ho-Ping was half-asleep when we arrived. He had taken off his shirt and with his half-closed eyes and naked belly he looked like some custodial god. He recognized me in the back seat and after an unintelligible greeting through his few remaining teeth, he waved us on.

There were no lights on in our part of the building and I groped my way up the narrow concrete steps to the second floor. We hadn't thought to lock our door and for the first time I felt a chill of fear as I pushed open the door and slid my hand over the wall searching for the light switch. Before I went to bed I checked the door again to be sure it was locked before I turned out the lights. Although we always pushed back the curtains as far as possible to get the maximum air, tonight I left them closed; I felt less vulnerable that way. Even so it took me hours to get to sleep. I was going to miss Anneke more than I had realized.

Her first phone call from Hong Kong was reassuring: Kurt had a broken leg, several broken ribs and a possible concussion but there seemed to be no internal injuries. Although he was in pain he was quite clear and conscious. Kurt's parents had decided to wait until after Christmas to fly in. Since he was in no danger they thought it better for them to remain at home with the younger children for the holiday. Anneke would stay on, of course, at least until they came.

Christmas Eve I taught all day with a program heavier than usual for I had been asked to cover two of Anneke's classes until the end of the semester. That evening I decided to walk the few blocks to the parish church for Midnight Mass. It was not something I anticipated with any eagerness. The hot, stuffy church, the cacophonous voices, the unfamiliar music–what had this to do with the Christmas I had always celebrated with so much joy?

In the church I noticed a scattering of Ho-Ping students but there was no one I knew well. In the front pew were two elderly teachers, converts from the Mainland, and behind them a young man from Berlin via Tokyo. The real surprise for me was on the far side. There, sitting by herself, her feet drawn up on the kneeler and her hands clasped in her lap was Mei-Lan. She seemed very small and young, sitting there in her school uniform, her hair pulled back into two braids.

I was suddenly filled with compunction. How terrible that I had let myself be so darkened with suspicion. In my distrust I had created an unreal Mei-Lan–a schemer, versed in intrigue and without scruples. Yet here she was, small, shy, fragile, waiting for Midnight Mass to begin. I looked over at her and smiled and she smiled back.

So Mei-Lan was a Catholic. It surprised me although I was not sure why. She was not a boarder and I wondered if she had come alone through those dark perilous streets on her bicycle. I would have to wait for her after Mass and find out how she was getting home.

From time to time I looked over but Mei-Lan never returned my gaze. She held the appropriate music in her hand and followed all the ritual movements but there was something withdrawn about her as though she was not sure she belonged. She did not receive Holy Communion and when I turned at the final blessing Mei-Lan was gone.

I felt strangely deprived and disappointed by her absence. Perhaps I had hoped in some way to make up for my suspicions, to salve my conscience with Christmas good will. But whatever had drawn her to the Christmas Mass had not kept her. As I left the church I walked slowly, thinking perhaps to see her bicycle. But the streets were empty.

On Christmas morning I knew that I couldn't stay at Ho-Ping all day. Mom and Pop and Tom had called early in the morning–fearful that they would miss me if they waited any longer. So, in fact, there was nothing to wait for and nothing much to do except plod through the 1300 dull pages of a Michener mammoth that I had picked up in the international book store.

When Anneke called a little later she was surprised that I wasn't getting ready to go down to Kan-Ting as we had planned. "Oh, go ahead, Les, you have our reservations; you might as well use them. Anyhow, there's no point in staying at Ho-Ping all day. It's too dreary. You'll enjoy the bus, I promise you–full of local color!"

She was right, I knew, and by mid-morning I was out on the highway trying to flag down a taxi. It took forever before one stopped and then the driver misunderstanding my limping Chinese, took me to the train station instead of the bus station. When, finally, I arrived, the bus on which we had reservations had already pulled out of the gate. The next bus, even if I were able to get a seat, would get me to Kan-Ting so late that it would be almost time to return home. But now that I was this far I couldn't bear to go back to Ho-Ping. I looked around to see what other possibilities there were–limited, of course, by the fact that most of the signs were unintelligible to me.

Scheduled for a departure in thirty minutes was a bus for Tainan. Anneke and I had gone there one Sunday and had found it an interesting city. Smaller and older than Taipei, it was a city filled with Taiwanese history with some of its temples among the most beautiful and ancient on the Island. I had remembered it as a friendly, happy city but clearly my impressions had been colored by Anneke's company. But now as I made my way out of the bus station and began to wander through the streets alone, I felt alien and embarrassingly visible. As I walked through the courtyard of the old Confucian temple, three little boys were convulsed with laughter at the sight of me. Anneke would have laughed back and said something in Chinese which would have convulsed them further. I could do neither and I walked on as though I hadn't noticed.

I searched in vain for a place to have lunch, but I was intimidated by the noise, the bustle and my inability to speak loud and fast enough to get served. Finally, I wandered into the outdoor market, deciding that I would buy some little cakes and fruit and eat them as I walked along. As I picked up my package, I turned suddenly and bumped into a woman bending over a stall of mantous, the heavy steamed Chinese bread I had never had the courage to try. "I beg your pardon," I said, the English phrase slipping out without my thinking.

She straightened up and looked at me. "Madame Hsu!" I said. Although it was a holiday she was as formally dressed as if she were in her classroom. While the other shoppers pushed and shoved in their bright T-shirts and dirty plastic sandals, Madame Hsu stood alone in her dark dress and polished shoes.

For a minute she said nothing. I wondered if seeing me here, out of context, had confused her. But then she bowed and almost smiled. "Miss Spendler. I would not expect to see you here. You have come for the holiday?"

Yes, I had come for the holiday–just for a few hours.

"And your friend, Miss Schaeffer, she is here?"

Clearly the news about Anneke hadn't filtered down to the Chinese department.

"Miss Schaeffer had to go to Hong Kong; a friend of hers was in a bad accident there."

She nodded but didn't ask anything else. The Chinese, I had discovered, didn't like to talk about accidents or death. "You have come to visit friends in Tainan?"

"No, I just came by myself, on the bus."

"All alone?"

I nodded, suddenly overwhelmed by the loneliness I had been trying to keep at bay. What a rotten, terrible way to spend Christmas, sloshing around in the mud of a Chinese street market, eating little cakes filled with mysterious substances for Christmas dinner. But I knew better than to cry in front of the indomitable Madame Hsu and I turned away until I could blink back the tears. But when I looked up Madame Hsu's face had softened, the lines around her mouth were less pronounced. She made no allusion to my being alone but guided me a little farther along the narrow alley.

"Have you seen the rest of the market?" she asked. "It is quite interesting." She toured me skillfully, in and out of little alleyways, into dark little stores, hardly bigger than closets but teeming with everything imaginable–beautiful materials, buttons of every shape and kind–past hawkers guarding mountains of socks and sneakers piled on rubber sheets, through to a tiny corner where chop makers shaped the intricate designs for the seals demanded by their clients, and on to the area where birds in their small cages hung from every available space.

"Have you had your dinner?" she asked when we emerged on the other side of the market.

"No, I was going to eat some little cakes I bought . . . ." but I suddenly realized my package was gone. "I must have put them down some place," I explained. "I'll go back and try to find them. Please don't trouble yourself. I'm sure you want to get home."

For the first time Madame Hsu smiled. "I think your little package is well eaten by now." She hesitated and then said, "Perhaps you would be so kind as to have tea with me. My home is only a little distance away."

I was too surprised to demur. "I would be honored," I said.

Even now I can still evoke with extraordinary clarity the afternoon spent with Madame Hsu. She lived on the third floor of one of those concrete boxes which seemed to be the constant in Taiwanese architecture. The room we entered had only two small windows. Against the wall was a bamboo couch covered with a quilt. On the other wall was a small recess which housed a two-burner hotplate. The rest of the room contained only a small table, two straight chairs, and an oval rattan rug which covered the middle of the concrete floor.

But the walls were startling. Even in the dim light the scrolls which covered them were clearly of exquisite calligraphy. My own shapeless efforts had taught me to appreciate the skill which produced such work.

"How beautiful," I said, as I walked closer to the wall to examine them. "Are they yours?"

"My father's."

She turned on the bare overhead bulb.

I walked from one to the other. The sure fluid strokes were like music.

"He was an artist?" I bent over to read the signature and see if I could find a date. "Did he live here in Taiwan?"

"He lived in Hangzhou. It is our native place."

My students always talked about Hangzhou when I asked them what city in China they would most like to visit. "The beautiful city by the lake," I said.

Again she almost smiled. "The beautiful city. We have a saying in China that if you live in Hangzhou there is no better place for you to go except to heaven. Please be seated; we can talk about the scrolls later. I must get some water for the stove."

I looked around but could see no source of water in the room. Madame Hsu took her pitcher and opened a door that had been hidden behind a huge scroll. She closed the door behind her but even so I could hear the murmur of voices. When she came back she said nothing but put the water on to heat, taking some of the things she had bought at the market and putting them into a container on the other burner.

I knew as I watched her that very soon I was going to have to ask to go to the bathroom. I felt awkward especially if there was someone sick in the next room. Meanwhile I walked about, examining the scrolls more closely and looking at the several photographs on the small table. They were all in black and white, framed in thin bamboo except for one of a middle-aged couple in an elaborate gold frame.

"My parents," Madame Hsu explained.

"And this one?" I asked, taking up a small photograph of two children about ten years old. They were the same height and had identical haircuts. The boy was smiling widely, clearly enjoying the experience but the girl was looking straight into the camera, her eyes focused on whatever old-fashioned mechanism was being used.

"My brother and I."

"You look almost identical."

"We were. We are twins."

"Are you really? I'm a twin, too." I was thrilled by the coincidence and suddenly I felt Tom powerfully present to me. "It's wonderful to have a twin brother, isn't it?" I asked.

The expression that passed over Madame Hsu's face was one I shall never forget–and one I shall never be able to describe. It was sadness, anger, envy, longing. I had never seen an expression quite so revealing–certainly not from someone so controlled as Madame Hsu–and I looked away, bewildered and even a little frightened.

She said nothing but turned back to the stove. The water had begun to boil and I knew that it was now or never to make my request for a bathroom.

"I wonder if I might use a bathroom, Madame Hsu?" I asked.

For a moment she gave no indication that she had heard me. Then she turned the dial down under the water and arranged two rice bowls at the side of the stove. When she turned, she didn't look at me but nodded toward the door.

"Please, this way. You must go through my brother's room."

She opened the door and walked ahead of me into a room dark and suffocating. The two opaque windows were closed and shades drawn over them. The air was heavy and damp like an underground passage that had been sealed off for a long time. In the corner with his back to the window, his head resting against a pillow, sat Madame Hsu's brother. It was hard to believe that this was a living body. He looked like a figure made of paper. His hands lay spread in his lap but they seemed to have no substance. Had I shone a light on them I would have expected the light to shine through.

Madame Hsu spoke to him but I caught only a few words explaining that I was a teacher from Madame Hsu's college. He opened his eyes and looked at me and despite his sister's protestations he struggled to his feet. He stood before me, a wraith in the black soutane and Roman collar of a Catholic priest.

"This is Hsu Fu," Madame Hsu presented, "my brother, Father Hsu."

He bowed and spoke, to his sister rather than to me. Like everything else about him, his voice was made of paper.

CHAPTER V

"Father Hsu wishes you to know that it is an honor to have you in our home," Madame Hsu translated.

"Please tell him," I said, trying to clear the rasp from my own throat, "that I am honored to be here."

"He understands you," said Madame Hsu. "His English is very good but he does not have the strength to speak it."

She turned again and spoke to Father Hsu and he eased himself into his chair and closed his eyes.

"You will find the bathroom over there to the left," she directed me, and then started back to the outer room.

I closed the door behind me. It was a Western toilet and a Western shower but so narrow that twice I knocked my elbow against the wall. When I finished I opened the door a crack and stared into the next room. Two of the walls were draped in black material and pinned to them were dozens of photographs–men and women, mostly between thirty and forty, two or three in clerical garb, a few in Western business suits. Through each photograph was drawn a diagonal cross. In the corner, pushed against the wall, was a small table, covered with a white cloth. On each side was a candlestick and in the middle a silver chalice. The soft silver was battered and the chalice tilted precariously but the metal was polished to perfection. Above it hung a crucifix. The cord that held it had slipped so that it hung askew, one arm reaching down toward the table.

An altar, I realized–an altar prepared for Mass. I wondered what kind of ritual was enacted here and if there were ever a congregation beyond Madame Hsu. I tiptoed through the room but Father Hsu gave no sign that he noticed me. He was lying in his chair, as he had been before, his hands flat in his lap.

Madame Hsu had fixed glasses of tea and a bowl of steamed dumplings. "It is not Christmas dinner, as you are used to it, but it is a little better than eating cakes in the market."

I tried to smile and thank her but I could do neither. As I sat on the couch the image of those dark walls and that insubstantial figure marked everything I looked at, like some powerful after-image of the sun.

Madame Hsu took up her chopsticks and put some dumplings in my bowl as though what I had witnessed did not exist. She mixed the sauce for the dumplings carefully and offered it to me.

"In 1949 when the People's Army came, my brother stayed behind to help my parents. He had been ordained just six years and had very firm faith in God but God did not choose to hear his prayers. My parents were killed, also my first brother and second sister. Father Hsu was imprisoned. They had many questions to ask him about our family and our property. Also about his Western education and his religion. It took a long time for them to get all the answers but in the end he told them."

She paused, her chopsticks poised above her bowl. "Finally after a long and difficult time my cousin was able to arrange his escape. He felt it more important for the priest to live than for himself."

"And the photographs?" I knew without asking.

"Members of our family. Chinese families are very large, you know. If you looked carefully you would see a name and the date of death. My brother keeps careful records."

"Is he . . . " I stumbled, "does he . . .?"

"Still fulfill his role as priest? Only here. As you see, he has not strength to do more. Sometimes he wishes to say a Mass for those who have died. He does it in his room. You have seen the altar. There is no need to tell the bishop. I am his assistant."

"And his twin." It was beyond my imagination. That frail ancient figure and this sturdy dark-haired woman with her will to conquer. Twins.

"Yes, his twin. Six minutes apart our father told us." She poured more tea. "Some find it easier to survive than others. Sometimes I think he had too much faith. He thought God would always save him. If you grow up a girl in China you learn early that you must save yourself. You are not of so much value that someone else will save you."

She mixed more sauce and put another dumpling in my bowl.

"When you have finished, I think we must go. I'll take you back to the bus; you'll never find your way from here. Even so, it will be almost dark when you get back to Ho-Ping."

That night, tired as I was, I wrote in my diary. I had to get it all down before time blurred it.

> "I think I've never felt sadness the way I did today. I saw death in its worst form, a kind of leprosy of the spirit. It was terrifying to hear Madame Hsu say of her brother that he had had 'very firm faith in God' as though that was what had destroyed him.

So much death and now he can think of nothing else, as though it were the thought of the dead that keeps him alive. And then there's Madame Hsu who has chosen to live–to live for both of them. I keep seeing me and Tom and wondering which of us would choose life and which of us would turn to paper. It wasn't simply suffering, even the physical violence, that unnerved me: it was the after-effect of suffering which obsessed and disoriented me."

I closed my notebook but I couldn't turn away from what I had recorded. I sat for a long time with the door open to a world I had never imagined.

CHAPTER VI

The weeks between Christmas and Chinese New Year were wild with activity. Final examinations took on a hysteria which I had never before experienced. To my students, grades meant everything. They determined their futures economically and socially and especially the students in their final year responded in a kind of frenzy. Their poise, their ritual politeness, were abandoned in their feverish determination to place well. They pushed and shoved their way in the halls, bolted out the door as soon as the bell had rung, and even dashed by me on the stairs without acknowledgement.

In addition to all this was the increasing concern as the day for the National Speech Contest drew near. Every available minute was spent coaching students in their prepared speeches until I knew them by heart. I practiced their vowels, I rehearsed their "r"s, encouraging them when possible to substitute words free of the unpronounceable consonant. "Be specific, talk about mangos or bananas not fresh fruit," I advised Chiang Yu-Be after trying in vain to correct her from saying "flesh flute."

Every day when classes were finished at 4:30 I gathered the finalists and fired topics for impromptu speeches at them. According to the rules they had three minutes to prepare and one minute to give their speech. This was where Mei-Lan shone. She was poised and inventive with that indefinable quality which bridges the gap between speaker and audience.

The pace exhausted me and some nights I lay down as soon as I got home, leaving supper until nine or ten o'clock and then satisfying myself with ersatz Chinese noodles or cheese and crackers and a mango taken from the trees beside the dormitory building. Only then did I begin the labor of correcting papers and preparing for the next day's classes. It was an insane way to live but I could find no alternative and at least it kept me from realizing how lonely I was without Anneke.

She called every couple of days but the connection was often too poor to carry on a decent conversation. Kurt was coming along, she told me, although it was taking longer than they had anticipated. Mrs. Tauber and Kurt's older brother had flown in after Christmas but they had stayed only a couple of days. Neither of them spoke Chinese and there was really nothing they could do to help Kurt.

"What about you? Are you all right?" Anneke asked when she called two days before the speech contest.

"Dead with fatigue but otherwise OK."

"It's always that way before end of term. Just stick it out for another week and then you'll have a glorious five weeks of vacation. I hope you're going to go up to Taipei. It's lots of fun up there at Chinese New Year."

In fact I had made no plans. I had been too tired and too busy to think about vacation.

"Listen, Les, you can't stay there, at Ho-Ping. It wouldn't be good for you, really. The place will be deserted."

"There'll be some Vietnamese girls here; they have no place to go for the feast. Maybe we can do something together."

"That might be fun for the day but after that you have to get out. How about coming to Hong Kong? I'm not at the hospital all day; we could do some sightseeing. I'm a pretty good guide, you know; I lived here for almost a year."

"It sounds wonderful." Suddenly the thought of something fun, something unpressured and free, made me realize how hard these weeks had been.

"OK, then, let's do it. You'll have to get a dozen permissions. You better go to the police station right away. That will give them time to process everything." An insistent crackling had started on the line. "I'll call you Saturday night and find out how things are going."

Anneke had forgotten that Saturday was the day of the speech contest and that I, as coach, was expected to go up to Taipei on an early morning train and stay with my students throughout the day. The disquiet that had never left me since that accusing piece of paper had slipped out of my folder had now grown into a heavy foreboding. I was filled with a sense of dread that had little to do with the success or failure of my students. It rose instead from a far deeper core: teasing doubts about my own integrity. Every time I saw Fong Li-Hwa–and she sat before me three hours a day–I questioned the decision I had made. Perhaps she was superior to Mei-Lan. Perhaps I had been influenced by that insidious little note. Perhaps it was Li-Hwa who deserved a place among the finalists. I told myself a dozen times a day that my decision had been made in good faith but it did not free me from doubt. My attitude toward Mei-Lan only increased my anxiety. Of all my students she was the one who captured my interest. I could hardly understand my attraction and yet it was there. Even though she did nothing to signalize herself, yet I was conscious of her as I taught, aware of her responses, curious about what she was thinking.

And then the morning before the trip to Taipei I was suddenly freed from my role as coach. I woke up with the most massive cold I had ever experienced. My voice was entirely gone, my eyes were swollen and my nose was running. I looked wretched and it was clear I was running a fever. Even the dean agreed that I was in no condition to accompany the students to Taipei. My suggestion that I be replaced by Miss Ruby Gao was accepted without demur.

Ruby was young and pretty and was, I thought, snubbed by the members of the English Department. Miss Gao taught Business English and was, therefore, officially part of the Commerce Department. In fact, her English was far superior to some of those who taught the upper division, but she was in many ways an anomaly. She had been born in Jersey City where her father had worked in a restaurant. When Ruby was eight he died suddenly and her mother, feeling lonely and frightened, had brought Ruby and her two young brothers back to Taiwan. Although Ruby had spent only a short part of her life in America, those years had made a lasting impression.

There was something free and sparkling about her that set her apart. Although she had a Chinese name under which she was officially registered, she insisted on using her American name whenever she could. Her father, she explained, had wished her to be a "real American" and since she had been born on the first day of July he had named her after her Western birthstone.

For the next two days I slept, getting up only to boil

drinking water and make some tea and rice. It was as though I had been anaesthetized. When late Saturday afternoon Anneke called I could hardly pull myself into consciousness.

"Les, you sound terrible; what's the matter?"

"Just a cold. Nothing bad."

"What are you doing for it?"

"Sleeping mostly."

"I hope you're not running a fever. What about the speech contest? I thought it was today."

"It is. Ruby Gao took my place."

"Are they back yet?"

"It's only five o'clock here. They won't get back until nine at least."

"I'm sure they'll do well. Ho-Ping always does. Listen: about Hong Kong. Have you made arrangements?"

"Not yet. I've been too busy. I'll do it first thing next week."

"OK. But don't put it off. There's always so much red tape, even for foreigners."

"I'll do it Monday after school. How is Kurt?"

Anneke hesitated. "Oh, Les, I don't know. Sometimes I get worried. He's so listless and sleepy. They say his head injury is all right but it frightens me a little to see him like this. I'm not sure what to do and there's no one to ask. If he isn't much better next week I'm going to ask his father to come and make some decisions."

It was the first time I had ever heard Anneke sound depressed. I was glad I had made the decision to spend my holiday in Hong Kong. "Anneke, call me next Wednesday evening," I suggested. "By that time I'll have all my permissions and I can tell you what flight I'll be on."

Anneke's call had roused me from my lethargy. I took a shower and washed my hair and then fixed a proper supper for myself. The food tasted good. Although my head was still congested, my throat was less painful. It was clear that I was much better. I put on my robe and sat reading the issue of *Newsweek* Tom airmailed to me every week. I was just about to turn out the light when I heard someone coming up the steps and then heard a knock on the door. It was Ruby Gao.

"I bother you?" she asked.

"No, of course not. Come in." I turned on the overhead light and motioned her toward a chair. Ruby was aswirl in a full skirt of green satin, topped with a bright black and orange sweater. She was nothing if not flamboyant.

"No, no, I not stay. Only to bring you good news from Taipei. Ho-Ping win two medal–first and third. Everyone very happy."

"Who?" I asked. "Who won?"

"Gold medal for Wu Hsiao-Li. Everybody expect this. She always very best. For second come boy from Industrial College. Not so good but must always be boy. For third medal comes big surprise. You want to guess?"

I shook my head.

CHAPTER VI

"O.K. I tell you: third medal go to Li Mei-Lan."

She wandered on, telling me the order of the day, the topics of the impromptu speeches, praising the excellent performance of the students from Ho-Ping. "Now I go," she said finally. "You sleep very happy tonight. You bring great success for our school."

But, of course, I did not sleep happy. I hardly slept at all. The faces of the eight contestants from which I had chosen the finalists kept passing before me. Of the eight two shone with a special light: Fong Li-Hwa and Li Mei-Lan. It was Mei-Lan's face that kept me awake–a face at once tranquil and controlled yet unusually vigilant. And yet fascinating as she was to me I knew that Mei-Lan would not be considered a Chinese beauty. There was something wilful about her, something that escaped from perfection as though she saw perfection as bondage. It was intelligence that set her apart–a special kind of knowing that from time to time slipped out of her secret store of subtlety. Mei-Lan of all of them, it seemed to me, had the acuity always to see what might be to her advantage and the will and daring to carry it out.

But then a counter-image rose before me. I remembered her as she had sat at Midnight Mass: very shy and quiet in her school uniform, her head bowed, her hands folded on her knees. That image had endeared her to me. She had touched me that night and I had experienced an unexpected disappointment when she had disappeared without a word.

I sat up in bed, hot and restless. I was thirsty but the thought of braving the waiting mosquitoes for a cup of tepid water was too much. I turned my pillow over and rested my cheek against it. When finally I slept I didn't dream of the speech contest; I dreamed instead of a tall glass of clear water with ice cubes tinkling against the rim.

The next morning was Sunday. Although my head was still stuffy, I was feeling sufficiently better to go to the parish church for Mass. It wasn't a service I enjoyed but today I felt I needed to get out and stretch my legs. Ordinarily I walked but when I got downstairs I saw Anneke's Honda leaning against the wall and decided to use it. Although I had never driven on the main roads without her, I decided that there wouldn't be much traffic early on a Sunday morning. I unchained the machine and was pushing it out from under the stairwell when I saw a shadow against the wall. I turned too quickly, scratching the handlebars against the wall. There standing at the entrance was Mei-Lan.

For a moment I hardly recognized her. Her dress was a far cry from the staid blue uniform in which I had always seen her. She was wearing a pale blue silk pleated skirt, a full-sleeved white blouse plentifully embroidered with flowers, and a soft blue shawl draped gracefully over her shoulders.

"I come too early?" she asked. "I frighten you?"

"I guess, a little. I hadn't expected to see anyone here, especially not a lovely vision in blue."

"Vision" was too much for her and she smiled that generic smile which I had learned was the polite response to incomprehension.

"I would invite you up to my apartment but I'm on my

way to church."

"Because it's Sunday?"

"Yes, I'm a Catholic and we must go to church every Sunday. I think I saw you at church for Christmas Mass," I continued. "But you're not a Catholic, are you?" She shook her head. "Do you go often?"

"First time. I thought it would be pretty for Christmas and I like to hear the music. The songs are very nice." She hesitated. "Were you glad to see me there?"

The question caught me off guard and before I could answer, Mei-Lan said, "You smiled at me; you remember?"

Of course I remembered that I had smiled, that it had given me pleasure to see her there. But Mei-Lan, it seemed to me, was saying something more, investing the occasion with disproportionate significance. Instead of answering, I turned the subject.

"I'm glad to have a chance to congratulate you on your medal. We're all very proud of how well you performed yesterday. You've brought honor to your school. The third prize is very excellent especially when there is such high competition."

She looked down. "I think other girls from Ho-Ping speak better. I don't know why the judges pick me."

I had learned to pay no attention to such modest protestations. "I'm sure Miss Gao was very pleased."

For a moment Mei-Lan said nothing and then she looked straight at me with that sharp intelligence which had first identified her for me. "I thought you would come. Everyone expected."

It was more than an expression of regret; it seemed to me to be a subtle accusation.

"I had a terrible cold," I said. I couldn't keep the defensiveness out of my voice. "I stayed in bed all day."

"But now you are better," she said, smiling at me.

"Yes, I'm much better." Why did I continue to read a second level into Mei-Lan's casual comments? "I wish I could ask you to stay longer, Mei-Lan, but I'll be late for church." I pushed Anneke's Honda out to the path and turned to say goodbye. "Do you live far from here?"

"Not far. A little bit over there," and she pointed toward the center of the city.

"How did you get here?" I knew Anneke would have invited her to hop up behind her on the motor bike but I wasn't that confident a driver.

"I borrow my brothers' motorcycle. I leave it by the dormitory."

We said goodbye and I went out along the dirt road at the back of the college and on to the main highway. I had hardly gone a half-mile when Mei-Lan passed me, sitting low on a powerful black motorcycle. Her skirt was pulled up over her knees and her shawl billowed out behind her. She swept by, confident and skillful, while the little Hondas on both sides cleared a path for her.

Later, I remembered that machine–its speed and power and the strong skillful hands needed to channel its force.

When Anneke called me the following week my plans for going to Hong Kong were complete. I had round-trip reservations, a plentiful supply of traveler's checks, and my exit visa was being processed. Ten days later Anneke met me at Kai-Tak airport.

"Was it beautiful coming in?" she asked. "It's one of my favorite sights, coming in like that over the harbor with everything all blue and silver. I think there's no place quite like it."

It had been only a month since she had left Ho-Ping but her German accent which had been barely perceptible was now quite noticeable. "I never speak English here," she explained, "only German with Kurt and Chinese to the doctors."

Anneke had brought us to a tiny Chinese restaurant lost in a narrow alley. "My father used to bring us here when we lived in Hong Kong," she explained when I asked how she had ever found it.

She nibbled at the edges of a fried dumpling and then put it down before biting into it. I realized as I watched her that it had not been simply the effect of the lights at the airport: Anneke was considerably thinner and very pale. I didn't ask about Kurt. I figured she'd tell me when she was ready.

She told me that night as we sat on her bed at the Lutheran Church Hostel where Anneke had gotten rooms for us. Although Hong Kong was warm during the day, once the sun went down it was surprisingly chilly and we both sat wrapped in blankets.

"Kurt's gone back to Germany."

I reached to put down my cup of tea but before I could say anything, Anneke said, "I suppose I should have told you. It wasn't fair to bring you here like this but it was all so sudden."

She wiped the tears away like a boy, with the back of her hand. "He left two days ago, so he's home in Mainz now."

"What happened?" It didn't seem likely that they would let him fly to Germany if he had gotten worse.

"Nothing really. Kurt was just the same. The doctor kept saying, 'Fine, fine.' But Kurt wasn't getting any stronger and he would sleep for hours. The bones in his legs were healing but it worried me to see him always so listless. They said it would take time to get his strength back but it was already a month. I began to wonder if maybe the concussion was something more serious. I called his family every few days and last week his father said he was coming."

She stopped and wiped her eyes again. "So he came." She put her head down on her knees and sobbed. "It was so awful, Leslie. Kurt looked terrible the day his father came. And his father was so angry; he yelled at the doctor and the nurses–and at me. I know it was only because he was afraid. It was his son. And to see him like that."

"But you had done everything. Why would he be angry at you?"

"He said I should have demanded more explanation from the doctors, that I should have let him know how sick Kurt was."

"But you did."

"Yes, but perhaps I didn't say enough. I didn't want to frighten them and every day I thought, 'This day will be better; Kurt will get strong today.'" She reached in her bathrobe pocket for a handkerchief.

"So they arranged to take Kurt home. They were able to get special equipment for the plane. They made only one stop, at Abu Dhabi, and then went straight to Frankfurt. From there it was easy to get him to Mainz."

I reached over and gave her another handkerchief out of my suitcase.

"Are you angry that I didn't tell you?" she asked.

"Of course not. I'm glad I'm here; it must have been awful for you to be here alone. Didn't you want to go back to Germany with Kurt?"

"Mr. Tauber didn't want me."

I started to protest but she shook her head.

"No, he didn't want me, not right then. He is a good man and we are friends and later perhaps he will tell me how sorry he is for how things happened. But I could not have gone with them. I really could not."

We stayed up talking until we were both half-asleep but even after we had gone to bed I could hear Anneke turning restlessly. Despite our efforts, the next two days were far from relaxing. Anneke was an expert guide and she shepherded me around all the obvious places of interest. We wandered down Nathan Street, took the ferry over to the Island, had lunch on the floating boats at Aberdeen. Hong Kong was every bit as curious and exotic and exciting as I had imagined and I knew Anneke was glad to have me with her, but a cloud hung over us which neither of us could dispel.

"Anneke, for heaven's sake, why don't you call and find out how Kurt is?" I asked the evening of our second day.

"I don't know; I feel funny."

"But you're Kurt's fiancée. Surely Mr. Tauber is not so unreasonable that he would resent your calling. He must understand how worried you are. Anyway, by this time he's probably regretting what happened."

I couldn't imagine that he wouldn't have called her by now and I knew she wondered, too. Every time the phone at the end of the hall rang she ran for it; but so far it was never from Germany. She stirred her tea round and round, although she had put no sugar in it.

"Maybe I'm afraid. Maybe they have found something wrong that the doctors here didn't see. Then I don't think I could forgive myself."

"But it wasn't your fault," I argued. "You did everything you could."

"Maybe not enough," she shrugged, "not enough to make him better." It was as though something had turned her to wood. Nothing I said could move her. Twice when I woke during the night I heard her crying and I made up my mind to do something that would move her to action.

The next morning when she came back from her shower, I said, "Anneke, I'm going to ask you a question and I want an immediate answer. No second thoughts. Understood?"

She nodded.

"OK. If someone gave you a ticket and ordered you to be on a plane to Germany by this evening, how would you feel?" She didn't have to answer; the answer was clear.

"Then that's what you're going to do."

"Oh, Leslie, I can't; you know I can't."

"No, I don't know you can't. Why can't you? Do you have enough money? Do you have your passport? What else do you need?"

"What about school? I can't just leave."

"Look. You have three weeks of vacation left. Go home. See your family. See Kurt. Find out how he really is. There's no reason why you can't be back in time for spring term."

But even as I said it, my intuition told me that if Anneke left now she wouldn't come back no matter how things went for Kurt. All the bounce was out of her as though she had been tested beyond her resources. It wasn't a physical sickness but it was the kind of depletion that comes sometimes when one is out of one's native climate for too long.

"Do you really think I can?"

"Of course you can; why not?"

"I hate to leave you here. It doesn't seem right. I brought you over to Hong Kong and now I'm going to leave you."

"I always wanted to see Hong Kong. I would have come anyway even if you hadn't been here."

She smiled. "You don't have to lie. I can accept that you came because you are my friend."

"Will you do it, Anneke?"

"OK. I guess so." And then, with something of her old energy, "Sure. Why not!"

In the next six hours we got her reservations to Frankfurt, changed Hong Kong dollars to German marks, bought some little presents for her family and had a final Dim Sum lunch at the Emperor's Tiger. At 7:00 p.m. we said goodbye at Kai Tak. Anneke walked through security, I waved for the last time, and then took a taxi back to my hostel.

I was determined to stay on and see the rest of Hong Kong but it was no good. The weather had turned cloudy and there was no point in going up to the Peak. I took the bus downtown but instead of adventuring into new areas I found myself revisiting the places Anneke and I had been together. I have a terrible sense of direction and there was something ominous about those twisted little alleys veering in all directions that confused me hopelessly. The crowds, the hawkers, the ingratiating hands that tried to pull me into their stores all seemed sinister to me now that I was alone.

On the afternoon of the third day, burdened with presents I had bought, I looked up to see an arrow pointing to "McDonald's" and without a moment's hesitation I headed toward it. As I sat there drinking my milkshake, watching all the pale lonely Westerners seeking solace in the familiar, I knew that I had stayed long enough in Hong Kong. That afternoon I changed my plane reservations and twenty-four hours later I was back in Ho-Ping.

CHAPTER VII

VII

Even though Anneke had promised that she would be back at Ho-Ping in a couple of weeks I was convinced that once back in Germany she would stay. I could not imagine how I would get through the semester without her. It didn't help my spirits to be held up at Customs as they meticulously unwrapped and examined every purchase I had made. When they turned over a small cloisonné jewelry box, telling me that it must be confiscated because it was stamped "People's Republic of China," I was ready to cry. My explanation that I had not been to the People's Republic, that I had bought it in Hong Kong fell on deaf ears. It was not until a superior officer, hearing the argument, came over to the desk that my purchase was returned. His solution was simple: he inked out the offending stamp and handed my jewelry box back to me. The logic escaped me but I had no inclination to argue.

When we reached Ho-Ping the campus was in total darkness. Even the students' dormitory where some stair lights were usually kept on all night was completely dark. I dragged my luggage up the narrow stairway and then sat on the stone steps rummaging in my bag for my key. As I opened the door to our apartment my foot stumbled against something resting across the sill. I shoved it aside as I groped for the light switch and pushed my luggage into the room. As always when a light was switched on there was a sudden rush of cockroaches scurrying to their homes. In addition our geckos, Alphonse and Alphonsine, leaped from the window frame to take up their favorite perch on the ceiling.

The windows had been closed, of course, and the airlessness was sickening. I pushed them open as far as they would go and pulled back the drapes in all three rooms. I was dying of thirst but of course there was no drinking water. I put water on to boil, wondering how long before it would be cool enough for a pleasant drink. Suddenly I was too tired to care and after washing my hands and face and brushing my teeth carefully so as not to swallow any impure water, I pulled down my mosquito net and went to bed.

I slept luxuriously late and it was already uncomfortably warm when I got up. I made some coffee and ate a couple of stale soda crackers before beginning to unpack. There, wedged between my two suitcases, was the object I had tripped over the night before. It was a small square box, beautifully wrapped. I opened it carefully hoping to find some identification inside; but there was nothing except two smaller packages, containing cassette tapes of Chinese music–one of popular contemporary songs and the other a classical flute concerto. I had already received gifts from the English Department and I wondered if this had been meant for Anneke.

I finished unpacking, leaving a large bundle of clothes at the front door to be taken to the laundry later. I was just coming out of the shower when I heard a knock at the door.

"Who is it?" I asked, tying my robe in place. There was no answer and I asked again, "Who's there?" I could hear a voice but couldn't identify it. I opened the door a crack and there stood Li Mei-Lan. She had on a red flowered skirt and a navy T-shirt with white letters reading "GO FOR IT." The shirt, sizes too big, hung loosely over her shoulders and breasts making her seem even smaller and younger than she was.

"Mei-Lan, what a surprise! Is something wrong?"

But Mei-Lan was imperturbable. "Nothing wrong. I come to see if you find present."

Her "r"s were indistinct and for a moment I missed her meaning.

"I leave you present," Mei-Lan explained again.

"Oh," I said, "the tapes. Thank you very much. They're lovely."

"You listen?"

"Not yet. I haven't had time. I only got back last night." I wanted to sound grateful but instead I was sounding defensive. Mei-Lan smiled but said nothing.

"How did you know I was back today?" I asked.

"Oh, I come every day. I watch your window. When they open I know you come back."

"You came every day?" I could hardly credit it.

"Not far to come. I ride my bicycle."

Perhaps not far but why? Why on earth would anyone ride a bicycle through that traffic to look up at my closed windows? She must have caught my puzzlement.

"I come to see if you find present."

"Yes, I found it as soon as I got here. I'm sure the tapes

are very beautiful."

"It's the flute you say you like one day in class. I remember so I can buy for you."

"But how would I have known it was from you? You didn't leave any card with your name."

She nodded. "So if somebody else find they not know who sent."

The implication was, of course, that anyone who noticed the package would trouble to look at the card. But even so, why would it matter? "But it was a very thoughtful thing for you to do, Mei-Lan. Why wouldn't you want anyone to know?" Mei-Lan's eyes met mine and once again I saw that look I had first seen the day I had set up my disastrous "court of law".

"Jealous," she said and lowered her eyes.

The word was at once ridiculous and chilling, hinting at realities that I was blind to. "Jealous? Just because you gave me a present? Why would that make anyone jealous?"

This time Mei-Lan did not look at me. "Because it make me special girl."

I could feel my irritation rising. I felt as though I had walked into a trap and didn't know how to extricate myself. I could hardly refuse Mei-Lan's gift but I had no intention of accepting her conclusion that this made her a "special girl". It was a stunning kind of bribery that was beyond my mastery.

The water I had put on earlier had begun to boil and I turned away without responding. "I was just going to fix a cup of coffee," I said. "Would you like to have one with me?"

She hesitated. "Very bitter?"

"Probably. How about tea, would that be better?"

She nodded, looking curiously around the room.

"I'm sorry it's so messy; I was just unpacking."

"Mezzy?"

"Not neat, not in order."

"Very neat." She got up and walked around the room. On the back of her T shirt was printed, "RED HOT POWER." "So big," she said, looking at me in amazement. "Only one person for this room?"

"Well, actually we have three rooms for the two of us, for Miss Schaeffer and me. Do you have sisters who share your room?"

"Two sisters, very small. Little one have one-year birthday tomorrow."

"And what about your brothers, are they little too?"

"Oh, no, very big. They marry now. I was youngest but then my mother die and my father take second wife."

So that was the explanation of the two babies. Mei-Lan had a step-mother. I wondered how happy her family life was. Anneke had told me that Chinese step-parents often made life very painful for their step-children. Perhaps this was the root of Mei-Lan's need to be a "special girl".

Before I could ask any more questions, Mei-Lan, leafing through a copy of *Newsweek*, asked me, "You like movies?"

"Some movies. Do you?"

"I like American. I like *Ordinary People.*"

I was surprised. "That's an old movie."

"Yes. They show in my brother's school."

"It was a very sad story," I said.

She nodded. "He wanted to suicide."

"Thank goodness he was saved. That would have been terrible for such a young person with his whole life to look forward to."

Mei-Lan was looking at me appraisingly and suddenly my response rang in my ears like empty clichés.

"When my uncle–Father's first brother–suicided my father said he did best thing. Otherwise whole family suffer shame."

"Mei-Lan, you don't really believe that, do you? Life is the most precious gift we have; how could it be better to throw it away? There's nothing so bad that we can't make up for it. What could be gained by your uncle's suicide?"

I knew that suicides were not uncommon but Mei-Lan looked so Western, sitting there in her American T-shirt and short skirt that the conversation seemed incongruous. But she stubbornly pursued her subject.

"At university when student fail examination sometimes he suicide."

"Oh, Mei-Lan, such a waste of life. Why?"

"For shame," she said and smiled.

Jealousy, shame. Words I had thought belonged to an ancient Chinese culture but here they were, changing people's actions and ordering their lives. I wondered when I would begin to hear about "revenge", the third of that classical triad.

The conversation lagged and when Mei-Lan finished her tea she stood up to go. "I go to work now," she explained. "You have film for develop? I can do for you. I work in camera store."

No, I had no film but it was nice of her to offer. We stood at the door and I thanked her again for the tapes. She started down the steps and then turned.

"You know Golden Phoenix Restaurant?" she asked.

I shook my head.

"Very beautiful. Maybe you have dinner with me?"

Another bribe to make her a "special girl"? Yet she looked so innocent and appealing that I could not say no. Instead I temporized. "Perhaps some day. Right now I have a lot of things to do because Miss Schaeffer is away. But it's very kind of you to ask me, Mei-Lan."

She did not press but nodded and continued down the stairs. I watched her walk across to the bicycle rack and mount her dusty black machine and ride out the gate.

I pulled the drapes to shut out the heat and made another cup of coffee and thought about Mei-Lan. I had never met anyone who set up such conflicting emotions in me. I knew that much of my negative response originated from that unsigned note identifying my "betrayer". But I had no proof that Mei-Lan was responsible and it was grossly unfair to judge her. As for wanting to be a "special girl", I suspected they all did in one way or another. Mei-Lan was simply tenacious enough to "Go for it"–as her T-shirt said–and naive enough to admit it.

After all, was her desire so unacceptable? Clearly she was not special at home. Her older brothers would always be favored before her and now, no doubt, her two baby sisters would get her parents' attention. Mei-Lan was conscientious at school, she had a job, and was probably responsible for much of the housework. Surely she needed to be special some place. And to be special to an American teacher would place her high on the ladder. Yet, strangely, this was just what she was guarding against. No one must know because only so could she ward off jealousy.

It was all too murky for me. One thing I had learned in my months at Ho-Ping: Chinese motivation was a far, far cry from my own.

VIII

Once the spring semester got underway I had little time to think about anything but work. In addition to teaching I had also been asked to coach the school play–a spectacular performance put on each year by the graduating class of the English Department. This year it was to be *Pride and Prejudice*. Although there were no boys to play the men's roles, still it seemed a better choice than *The Barretts of Wimpole Street* which had been the other possibility. Darcy was far more willowy and soft-spoken than the text suggested, but Elizabeth was tall and decisive with a rather fine accent. Mei-Lan was chosen for the part of Lydia-clearly a disappointment for her. She had had her heart set on playing Elizabeth rather than her flighty sister.

A teacher from the Chinese Department was in charge of costumes and staging and Ruby Gao was given to me as my assistant. Although her accent was not good enough to help with coaching the students' speech, she was a wonder at directing. Perhaps because she had so much life herself, she injected it into her actors. Under her guidance the staid Sue-Ling became a marvelously flirtatious Wickham and Mei-Lan developed a charming coquettish manner as Lydia.

Because of the play Ruby often stayed late. Sometimes we ate in my apartment or went down to the noodle house. On rare occasions I took Anneke's Honda; so long as I could get back by dark I was able to conquer my fears.

"How come you want to teach at Ho-Ping?" Ruby asked

one night over our noodles. It was incomprehensible to her that anyone would choose to leave the United States for Taiwan.

"Unlucky in love," I said, surprised at how painlessly I had come to think about Hal and what had happened to our engagement.

She laughed. "Oh boy, love is never lucky." Ruby's slang was generally a generation out of date.

"You're not very romantic," I chided her.

"Romantic is nice for having fun, not for being married."

"Spoken like a true Chinese." Ruby was the only one I could say things like this to, now that Anneke was gone.

"My grandparents say I speak like real American. They don't like how I speak."

"Do they live here in Chi-Yi?"

"You bet. We live all together–my mother, me, and Number Two Brother. Number One Brother work in Taipei."

"Isn't it hard for you, to live together like that?" Ruby seemed so independent that it was difficult to imagine her playing her part in a Chinese household.

She shrugged. "Chinese way."

"Are you going to teach at Ho-Ping again next year?" Ruby didn't strike me as a perennial teacher.

"Maybe. I like to go back to America but not enough money yet. I do translation after school; it helps a little." She looked at her watch. "For crying out loud! I'm late. My grandmother doesn't like if I'm out late. She still thinks like Old China."

We paid our bill and I waited while Ruby unlocked her bicycle. I waved as she rode down the highway tall and straight on her machine. It wasn't quite like having Anneke but Ruby was friendly and exuberant and it did me good to be with her.

It was just ten days before the production of *Pride and Prejudice* that Ruby disappeared. We often met in the cafeteria at noon but this day I looked for her in vain. As I was leaving I bumped into another member of the Commerce Department but when I asked her if Miss Gao was in her classroom I was met with a hard look and a quick shake of the head.

That afternoon after classes when I went to the lecture hall for rehearsal I found Hsieh An-Ling waiting for me. Miss Hsieh had been on the faculty at Ho-Ping since its establishment. She taught phonetics and reading to first-year students and although she applied each year for a promotion to a higher level, her request was never granted. When one listened to her English it was clear why. Although her pronunciation was passable, her grammar was disastrous. Perhaps because she realized her limitations, she was a hard and merciless disciplinarian. Sometimes when I passed her classroom I wondered why she was kept on at all–except for her seniority. Although we met seldom, when we did her manner was hostile and truculent.

She stood before me now more in the posture of a drill sergeant than a teacher. "I take place of Gao Laoshe," she said.

I was startled. "Of Ruby?"

She nodded. "Of Gao Laoshe." She would have nothing to do with Ruby's American name.

"Is Gao Laoshe sick?" I asked.

But she ignored my question. "You explain what I do and I take care."

"Will she be out all week?"

She didn't answer but looked straight ahead.

I tried again. "Is Gao Laoshe very sick? Will she be in tomorrow?"

"I take her place."

"Yes, I understand. But for how long will you take her place?" It would be disastrous to lose Ruby at this point in the production.

"I take her place every day."

"But I don't understand. Is Ruby, is Gao Laoshe very sick?"

"She has go away."

It was becoming like a comedy script. "Where has she gone?" What, I wondered, could have happened since the day before that would have caused Ruby to "go away", if, in fact, that was what she had done.

"She no more teach at Ho-Ping."

"No more teach at Ho-Ping?"

Hsieh An-Ling nodded.

"But why, what happened?"

Once again she avoided the question. "You tell me how and I help you."

I nodded. There was nothing else I could do. The students were already on our make-shift stage waiting for their cues.

Somehow I got through the rehearsal. When it was over, I went downstairs to the English office and picked up the books and papers I would need for the evening. Then I walked over to the East Wing and up to the third floor to the Commerce Department. Both teachers and students had already gone but the office was still open. I looked at the shelf where Ruby kept her books but it was empty. I edged through the narrow aisle and up to her desk. The small carved squirrel which I had given her and which she kept on her desk as a talisman was gone and so was the name plate which identified each teacher's desk. I opened the drawers. Nothing. I walked to the back of the room and opened the lockers where teachers occasionally kept a sweater or an extra pair of shoes. Ruby's locker was empty. I closed the door and walked through the empty building and across the quadrangle to my apartment.

At one point I had thought that Ruby might have been in a bad accident and that Hsieh An-Ling didn't know how–or didn't care–to tell me. But if that were the case no one would have cleaned out her desk so immediately and so completely. As I walked up the stairs to the apartment, I thought I heard a movement and when I looked up there was Mei-Lan sitting on the top step waiting for me.

Strangely, I felt no surprise. It was as though I had expected her. I unlocked the door and she followed me in, standing at the entrance, watching me as I put down my books. Neither of us made any explanations. It was clear that she knew what I had been doing.

"You look for Miss Gao," she said when I finally turned to face her.

"Is she sick?" I knew she wasn't. I knew that whatever had happened it was something worse than that.

Mei-Lan evaded the question. "I take you to her."

"Is she in the hospital?"

She shook her head. "You want to see her. I take you."

"You know where she lives?" An imperceptible nod. "Perhaps she would prefer not to see anyone." I was limping, trying to find an answer but Mei-Lan ignored the issue.

"You want to go?" she asked again.

Of course I did. I knew I had to. I reached up to the hook behind the wall to get the key to the Honda, but Mei-Lan stopped me. "Better to take bus. Very bad traffic now."

We waited in silence by the highway, watching the tipsy buses massed with people roar by. Mei-Lan nodded at me as one of them slowed down and she pushed me ahead of her up the steps. We were off, lurching down the road almost before the door had closed on us. For forty-five minutes we swayed and jerked as I tried to find enough space for both my feet. Finally Mei-Lan pushed me forward, shouting our way to the front of the bus and out. Then a dash across another street, narrower this time, and on to another bus. I could not see out the windows and by the time Mei-Lan again pushed me off I had no idea where we were. The streets here were narrow little alleys, muddy, with open sewers and two-storey concrete blocks of housing on either side. I followed in Mei-Lan's sure footsteps as we picked our way through muddy stretches, avoiding puddles and pieces of debris. Finally Mei-Lan stopped and pointed at a small, windowless house. When no one answered her knock, she banged louder and began to yell. The door opened a crack and I saw an elderly Chinese woman, dressed in black, her gray hair pulled severely into a bun. But before Mei-Lan could speak the door was slammed. Angry, she started to bang again and I put out my hand to stop her.

"Maybe Miss Gao doesn't want to see anyone."

Mei-Lan shook her head impatiently. "Only grandmother," she said and continued banging.

When the door opened a second time Mei-Lan was able to explain who we were, that we were friends of Gao Laoshe from her college; but the grandmother would have none of it. She eyed me hostilely, shaking her head at Mei-Lan's explanations. At the height of the argument, I saw a taller figure moving in the dark interior and then Ruby appeared behind her grandmother. She put her hands on her shoulders, gently trying to push her aside, speaking quietly, trying to stem the old woman's wrathful tirade. Finally, the grandmother wrenched herself free, and, still grumbling, shuffled into the next room.

When Ruby moved out into the light she alarmed me. She looked like someone suffering from high fever. Her eyes were bright and restless, her lids were swollen, and the deep hollows under her eyes were accentuated by her high cheek bones. I wanted to reach out and put my arms around her but she made no movement toward me.

She said nothing but motioned us to follow her into a small room crowded with large pieces of heavy wooden furniture in classical Chinese design. She gestured toward two chairs but Mei-Lan remained standing.

"I go to drink tea," she said; "I come back later."

Ruby nodded and closed the door. We sat together on a long wooden bench. Behind us was a narrow window which cast a triangle of light just in front of us. I reached out and took Ruby's hand. She didn't pull away but she made no responsive gesture.

"They tell you about me?" she asked. Her voice was husky and uncertain.

I shook my head. "No, nobody said anything; that's why I came."

She scowled. "They tell you I no longer teach at Ho-Ping?"

"No. I looked for you at noon and then when we started rehearsal Hsieh Laoshe came and told me she was taking your place. I asked her if you were sick but she didn't answer. Then I went to the Commerce Department and I saw that all your things were gone, so I got worried." I was doing my best to hide my anxiety.

"You ask that girl to bring you?"

"Mei-Lan? No, she offered. She was waiting for me when I got home."

Ruby nodded. For a while we sat in silence. She drew her hand away and folded her arms against her chest.

"They fired me," she said at last. "I'm all washed up."

CHAPTER VIII

The incongruity of the slang turned my heart. I hesitated to ask directly what had happened; instead I groped for something hopeful to say. "You can get another job," I encouraged. "Your English is good. Lots of schools or businesses would be happy to have you."

"No more. I can't get reference."

"Oh, Ruby, I'm sure that's not true." I couldn't imagine what could have happened that would keep her from getting a reference.

For the first time she looked straight at me and said something in Chinese. "You know what that means?"

I shook my head.

"In English you translate: 'a bad element; a no-good person'. You understand?"

Of course I understood. "Bad element" was an expression constantly in the papers: a label for people who were mixed up in drugs, men caught in extortion and bribery schemes, gangs of young hoodlums. Bad elements. But what could Ruby have to do with such things?

"They say I am an unmoral person, dangerous to have with young people." She turned away, trying to keep back the tears. "So I disgrace my whole family. You see my grandmother; she will not even open the door. She says she must hide her face now until she goes to her grave."

"But what did you do?" I no longer cared that the question might be considered intrusive

She shrugged. "Everybody know except you. If you knew Chinese you would know early this morning."

Early that morning, she explained, when she arrived at Ho-Ping she was immediately sent for by Colonel Sheng. The school had received a letter from a woman accusing Ruby of having adulterous relations with her husband and demanding that Ruby be publicly punished to redress the wrong she had committed. If the college did not act at once, she threatened, she would make a public declaration and cause a scandal for the school.

I was speechless. Talking had made Ruby calmer and now she reached out and put her hand on my arm. "You believe I would not do such a thing?"

"Of course I believe. The woman was lying; she couldn't have any evidence." The whole matter seemed outrageous.

"They have her letter."

"Yes, but that's no proof of anything. Anyone could write a letter like that. Any wife who wants to injure her husband, any woman who is jealous."

Ruby almost smiled. "Yes," she said, "jealous woman."

"But Ruby, if you have not done anything, she can't prove . . . ."

But she cut me off. "No need to prove; only to accuse."

"But that's insane. Can't you take her to court? Start a libel suit against her?"

Ruby looked at me in bewilderment. Clearly such action was beyond her comprehension.

I started on another tack. "What about the husband? Surely he won't let this happen to you?"

"He's a nice man. I worked for him a little. Remember, I told you I had extra job translating for a businessman? After school I went to his office, then when we finish he bring me home on his motorcycle. Some nights when it was late we stop for dumplings. But not many times. I only start to work for him this semester."

"But surely he'll stick up for you, swear that his wife's accusation is false."

She shook her head. "Then he lose job."

"But why would he lose his job if he isn't guilty of anything?"

"Scandal. Very bad for Chinese person. Nobody want to hire person who has been accused."

"Even if they are declared innocent?"

Again she shrugged. "He has been accused."

"So there's nothing you can do?"

She shook her head. "My grandparents very angry. They accuse my mother. They say if I did not live in United States this would not happen. They think Americans very unmoral."

There seemed no point in saying anything–at least not anything I could think of. Truth apparently didn't stand a chance against jealousy.

"What are you going to do?"

"I don't know. Maybe I can go to Taipei. Get small job where nobody know me."

"Do you have money?"

"Little bit."

Suddenly I remembered Vincent and his friends and wondered if they couldn't help her. "Listen, Ruby, I have some friends in Taipei. Americans. Let me give you their address. Maybe they can help you get a job."

She put her hand on mine. "Better not, OK? Not good for me now. My grandmother make it harder if she know I have American friend. Don't worry. Everything be A-OK."

We heard her grandmother coughing outside the door. Ruby smiled. "She try to listen in case we speak Chinese. Better you go now."

I wanted to put my arms around her, to do something to comfort her. Instead we bowed a little and she opened the front door for me. It was getting dark and the street was empty but Mei-Lan was standing at the end of the alleyway waiting to bring me back to Ho-Ping.

I thought about canceling my calligraphy class the next day but of course Madame Hsu had no phone and there was no way I could get in touch with her ahead of time. I hadn't slept much after seeing Ruby. The more I went over what had been done to her the more unbearable the injustice of it seemed. By the time I had finished my classes for the day and presented myself to Madame Hsu I knew I was very far from that "quiet contemplation" which calligraphy demanded.

I had not executed a dozen strokes before Madame Hsu took the brush from between my fingers and rested it slowly against the ink stone. She said nothing and I looked straight ahead. Our relationship had not changed appreciably despite the afternoon I had spent in her apartment. That insight into her life, that unflagging determination to triumph over suffering, awed me. The memory of that afternoon was still strong: the small austere room hung with those exquisite scrolls and then that other room where her brother lived in darkness and with the scent of death. Sometimes I tried to inject something personal into our lessons but she turned it aside, giving me no room to be other than her Western student.

Now she said, "You cannot hope to execute properly in such a state of distraction."

It was the same high, imperious tone she had used at the very beginning of our lessons. I thought we had at least advanced beyond this in the six months she had been teaching me and her tone angered me.

I turned quickly, my hand knocking the brush onto the desk. "I went to see Ruby Gao last night; I think it's terrible what has been done to her."

Madame Hsu was taking up the brush, wiping the spot it had left, and replacing it in its proper position.

I went on. "You know she lost her job, don't you? And I'm sure you know why."

She turned to look at me but still she said nothing. Her composure infuriated me. It was as though she had withdrawn beyond human response, as though another's suffering could not touch her.

"You can't believe that what happened to her was right, that doing a thing like that to someone young with her whole future ahead of her was fair. What that woman accused Ruby of didn't even happen and yet she was dismissed without any chance of explaining the truth. How can you let this happen and not do anything about it? Don't you care about anything but reputation? Doesn't truth mean anything to you?"

Suddenly all that had hurt, confused, bewildered me in the last six months was swept together in my passion for justice for Ruby. I flung my final dart with perfect aim. "How can you let this happen after all you've been through?"

For a moment the strength and purpose in that impassive face drained away and I saw a fleeting resemblance to her brother. But when she spoke her voice was clear and cool and perfectly in command.

"You are very sure in your judgments, Miss Spendler."

I shook my head, wanting her to understand. "It's just that I can't bear to have Ruby's life ruined over something that never happened."

"Miss Gao's life will not be ruined."

"But she's lost her job, her grandparents don't want her in their house, she'll have no references. She'll never be able to get her papers to go to America. I can't imagine what will happen to her."

"I'm sure you can't." The voice was drily amused but her face had regained its composure. "You would be surprised at what horrors we Chinese can survive." The words were full and terrible with experience. "I assure you," she went on, "that I do not approve of what happened to Miss Gao, but then I did not always approve of Miss Gao. I think she acted innocently but not wisely. It was foolish for her to go publicly to have supper with this businessman, to let him bring her home late at night."

I shook my head in opposition. "But for his wife to lie about her, to publicly humiliate her . . . . Surely you don't think that was right."

"Not right but to be expected."

She was taking my brush and putting it back in its case. "I think you have had a very nice life, Leslie; a nice life with nice people." I looked at her quizzically. "Only those who have not come close to evil can believe they can abolish it. My brother once believed as you. It was why he became a priest."

She shut the clasp on my brush case and covered the ink stone. "Today was not a good day for calligraphy. Perhaps next week you will do better," and she nodded to dismiss me. When I closed the door she was still sitting motionless at her desk.

IX

My conversation with Madame Hsu aroused in me something more painful than anger. I felt a kind of bereavement, a sense of loss. I had hoped that beneath her rigid exterior I would find compassion. But she had failed me. The lessons she taught were too harsh for my Western skin. What I was yearning for, although I had not yet acknowledged it, was friendship.

Although I thought I had adjusted well after Anneke's departure, I now realized the depths of my loneliness. Without Anneke I had few resources to count on and Ruby's dismissal had crippled me. I was losing my balance and I had to reach out for something to steady me. Mei-Lan was at hand, waiting.

I hadn't seen her since we had visited Ruby Gao but the following Friday as I was sorting papers to take home with me, a little note slipped out. "You wait for me after school," it said. It wasn't signed but the source was clear; no other student would have presumed to leave such a message. For a half-hour after the buses and Hondas and bicycles pulled out of the parking lot I sat at my desk with a sense of pleasant anticipation, the sense I used to experience when Anneke and I had planned something exciting at the end of a hard week.

Thus Mei-Lan and I spent our first evening together–the first of many, as it turned out. There was always a covert tone about them because Mei-Lan was insistent that they be kept secret from her classmates. None of my arguments could dispel her extravagant sense of jealousy. She was ingenious in finding little out-of-the-way places where we'd be unlikely to meet anyone from Ho-Ping: a little tea house in a back street, a small family restaurant, an American "coffee house" where we drank the sticky dark brew which passed for Western coffee. It tasted terrible even to me but Mei-Lan insisted on sharing it with me.

At first we talked about what all my students were most curious about: America. American movies, American clothes, American best-sellers.

"Who your favorite author?" Mei-Lan wanted to know and was shocked that it was not Stephen King or Danielle Steele. "Those books aren't real," I tried to explain to her. "They're not about real people. That's not how it is in America."

She was too polite to contradict me but I could tell I had made little impression.

"That's enough about life in America," I said one Saturday afternoon. "I want to learn more about your life, too– what it's like to grow up in Taiwan." But my questions received only limping answers.

"Hard to say in English," Mei-Lan pleaded.

And when I said, "Try, I'll help you," she simply shook her head.

"Not interesting to live in Taiwan."

"Of course it's interesting to live in Taiwan," I countered. "Everybody is fascinated about Chinese culture and Chinese people these days. Don't you know that?" She didn't answer but gave me one of her long appraising looks as she sipped her tea.

Looking back at those weeks in which Mei-Lan and I began to establish our friendship, I realize that part of their charm was that it was spring. Winter was hard at Chi-Yi, not because it was cold–although there were times when the winds blew down from Outer Mongolia and through the unheated buildings–but because it was so drab. The rains had stopped by the end of September and not a drop of moisture fell for the next five months. Everything became covered with a layer of brown dust–the leaves, the plants, the buildings, even a book left open on a desk for a few hours. It seemed that nothing would ever be clean and bright again. Then, suddenly, in February, out of that dry unpromising ground green things began to sprout. Plum trees had already flowered and now the pink and golden hibiscus had begun to bloom. There was movement everywhere: slow, imperceptible, but life-giving and I reveled in being a part of it.

Imperceptibly, too, my reserve and suspicion of Mei-Lan dissolved. It was intriguing to watch Mei-Lan–to see the things that excited her, the things that bewildered her. I felt as though I were engaged in a slow and intricate dance. Although the steps were new I felt confident because I thought that I was the one who was leading.

Mei-Lan became a preoccupation. When I read an interesting article in an American magazine, when my parents sent me clippings of new movies, when I remembered incidents from my childhood, instinctively I stored them up to share them with Mei-Lan. It was natural enough, I suppose, since there were no other channels for friendship.

CHAPTER IX

Even so, our relationship remained, for me at least, one of teacher and student. I thought of myself as her elder, her mentor, sometimes, even, as her savior. I offered her friendship, not as an equal but as a beneficent godmother, someone who could offer her a wider vision than Taiwan could provide.

In fact, we had little time to spend together–an hour or two late on a Saturday afternoon or evening; perhaps a little time on Sunday. School work was very heavy for me those days and Mei-Lan had her job as well as her duties at home. It was already too hot to enjoy walking but occasionally we found a bench by the lake outside the city where we could sit and talk.

"Saturday we have no school," Mei-Lan reminded me one afternoon when she waited for me after everyone had left. "Have you been to mountains?" she asked.

No, I hadn't. It was one of the outings Anneke and I had planned for spring vacation.

"You like to go? Very beautiful."

"I'd love to but don't you have to work on Saturday?"

"I take time off."

And so early on Saturday morning we boarded the bus for Taichung where we changed for another bus to take us up Taroko Gorge and into the central mountains and on over the narrow muddy highway to Tienhsiang. The trip was an unnerving alternation between exhilaration and terror. There was sheer delight in the awesome beauty of the wild green mountains and the tumbling streams a thousand feet below. For the first time I realized what Taiwan must have looked like before the ravages of factories and industrialization. It must indeed have been "Formosa"–The Beautiful One. But as the bus wheezed and slithered along the narrow track between the rocky wall on one side and the stark ravine on the other I was paralyzed with terror. There were no guard rails and it sometimes seemed to me that the rear wheels of the bus were slipping at the very edge of the road.

My hands were gripped tight in my lap and my teeth ached from being clamped so grimly. But ahead of me an old Chinese man slept peacefully and across from me a mother and child ate their lunch in slow enjoyment. Mei-Lan, too, was leaning back contentedly in her seat, looking out the window and admiring the beauty. It did not help me when she recited the number of workmen who had given their lives in the construction of the highway or explained that the red signs we saw every so often marked the spot of a fatal accident.

Mei-Lan had made reservations for us at the government hostel at Tienhsiang, a large modern building perfectly maintained. Our room was large, the largest I had ever seen in Taiwan, with four bunk beds and a very modern bathroom; but most wonderful of all was an immense picture window looking out onto the mountains. Not too far away, perched at the top of one of the closer hills, I could see the curved roofs of a large building.

"Buddhist monastery," Mei-Lan explained. "You like to go there?"

"Can we?"

"Yes, not far. Very nice."

And so, after lunch, we began our climb up the

mountains. The ominous rain clouds that had hovered over us on the bus had blown away and the sky was a pleasant blue-gray. Despite the modernization of the hostel and the little shrines and pagodas along the way, this was wild country, the mountains rising starkly arrogant, still untamed. Sometimes as I sat at my desk at Ho-Ping plodding through stacks of paper, my face and neck wet with perspiration, I had dreamed of just such a landscape–a dream of mountains, cool and pure where I would have space to breathe and be still.

At first we met a few other walkers but after a while we had the path to ourselves. At one point we came out of the woods onto a grassy plateau covered with gold and purple wild flowers. Two yellow finches swooped and dove among the pine trees. Everywhere black and orange butterflies, bigger than humming birds, rose from the grass, arced in short flights and then settled down again. After the dust and confusion of Chi-Yi it was the very image of an earthly paradise.

The Buddhist monastery, when at last we reached it, was quite deserted. It was a perfect setting for a monastery: high, vast, rising protectively over the small white houses of Tienhsiang. On two sides it looked down into the valley and on the far side the sharp mountain peaks rose, overshadowing the temple. I walked inside the temple precincts and stood watching the light from hundreds of candles flicker over the golden face of an immense Buddha. The vastness, the heavy incense and the dizzying lights were hypnotic and after a while I needed to escape into the fresh air. I found a smooth slab of rock where I could sit and look into the mountains. Although it was only mid-afternoon, the mist–gray and violet–was already beginning to settle over the western mountains.

Mei-Lan came from behind the temple and sat next to me. "You don't like?" she asked, looking at me quizzically,

"Of course I like it. It's beautiful. Why would you think I don't like it?"

"Not say anything," she observed.

"I'm enjoying the silence. Sometimes it's better than talking."

She nodded, pulling her feet up on the rock and clasping her arms around her legs. It was one of the few times when we had limitless time to talk and before the afternoon was over I surprised myself by telling Mei-Lan about my engagement to Hal and its unexpected ending. Clearly Mei-Lan found my recitation puzzling. She said nothing but sat scowling down at her feet.

Finally she asked, "Your parents ask you to leave their house?"

"Of course not. Why would they?" The tack was so unexpected that I hardly knew how to answer.

"You break up engagement. Not good for families. Maybe his family angry with you."

"I don't even know Hal's family. His father is dead and his mother is remarried and lives far away. I only met her once."

She was still scowling. "But your family suffer shame."

"No, Mei-Lan. It doesn't work like that. They were sad because they liked Hal and they knew I had been in love with him. But that was my decision. It didn't bring shame on them."

CHAPTER IX

She nodded but she still didn't look at me. "He suicided?" she finally asked.

"Hal?" The image of Hal, positive, ambitious, successful committing suicide because some girl had jilted him amused me. "That's the last thing in the world he would think of, Mei-Lan. He's probably found a much better catch already."

"Better catch?"

"Another girl, someone even nicer. Do you really believe that a man would commit suicide just because his engagement is broken?"

She nodded again. "Very bad disgrace for whole family." Then she looked up at me for the first time. "If girl, then even worse. No one want to marry her. She have no place to go."

"So you think maybe I came to Taiwan to hide my shame?"

She looked embarrassed but she kept on. "Maybe to find husband who doesn't know you, so maybe you can fall in love again."

I laughed. "I assure you, Mei-Lan, falling in love is the last thing I want to do right now. Maybe when I go back to America, maybe I'll meet someone . . . ."

"When you go?"

"Probably this summer after your graduation."

I was anxious to change the subject and I asked her, "What are you going to do after graduation? You've never told me."

"Find job, maybe in Taipei with business company. They like girl who speak English."

"Wouldn't you like to go to university?"

"I have to go to work."

"Because of your family?"

"My stepmother say I have enough time in school. Now I help out."

Mei-Lan was sitting, her head bowed, her cheek against her knees, her thick dark hair covering her face. A wave of affection swept through me, a strong desire to protect and shelter her and offer her some good thing.

"Mei-Lan," I said, "Suppose you were able to go to an American university and finish your degree. Would you like to do that?"

She looked up at me with something close to disdain. "Everybody like to do that," she said.

"Yes, I know. But it isn't possible for everybody. I'm talking about you."

"How could I do such a thing?" Her voice was defensive, as though she was afraid of being baited.

"Well," I said, "there are scholarships, you know." I had spoken impulsively and now I was picking my way tentatively. "In the college where I went they were always very happy to help Chinese students. Suppose you were able to get a scholarship and some help with your living expenses, would you like to go?"

She had turned away and was looking out over the

mountains. When she answered all the defense was out of her voice. "It is my dream," she said.

Thus began my active role as fairy godmother. I dreamed that she was enrolled in a good college. I dreamed that she would meet Tom and my parents, that they would help her along the way. And all the time I would be there, guiding, counseling, leading the dance.

Our shared ambition provided a focus for our friendship. It was the incentive Mei-Lan needed and her English improved dramatically. Meanwhile I pored over college catalogs, wrote letters, amassed information about requirements for Asian students.

One evening as Mei-Lan sat in my room reading the section of general information in a college catalog, she looked at me puzzled.

"In America all students go to church?"

I laughed. "Far from it. Why?"

"It say," and her finger searched for the place, "it say Sunday evening have Chapel Service. Chapel is other word for church."

"Yes, that's true and many colleges have opportunities for students to worship on Sunday but not everyone is obliged to go."

She was reading on. "Everyone Christian in America?"

"By no means. Many people are Christian but there are also Jews and Hindus and Buddhists–all sorts of religions."

"Which is best?"

"Best how?"

"Best to be."

It was one of Mei-Lan's unanswerable questions. "Well," I said, stumbling, "it's not really a question of what is 'best'; it's a question of what you believe in."

Clearly my explanation didn't satisfy and I tried again. "You see, it really doesn't matter what you are. Every religion is acceptable in the United States. You practice whatever you believe in. Whatever you were brought up in. OK?"

Mei-Lan nodded. "My step-mother is Buddhist. She fix little shrine in our house."

"And what about you?"

She shrugged. "Sometimes I go to Christian church."

"I know. I see you there."

"You like to see me there?"

"Well, yes, of course it's nice to see you there." I was stumbling worse than ever. "But that's not the point. You don't go to church to please someone. You go to worship the god you believe in. If you don't believe in the Christian god then you wouldn't go to a Christian church."

Again she scowled. "When we go to Tienhsiang you go to visit Buddha."

"Yes, but just to see. I didn't pray to Buddha. That's different."

"How you pray to Christian god?"

CHAPTER IX

I was ill-equipped to deal with Mei-Lan's interrogation. "Well, for example, I pray when I'm in trouble, when I need God to help me. Don't you sometimes need to ask someone to help you when things aren't going well and you can't manage by yourself?"

"Maybe nobody there to help."

It was Mei-Lan's basic scepticism. I had seen it slip out before: this bleak conviction that what one does with one's life must be done on one's own. This seemed to bring us to the end of the road. I could think of nothing to add and Mei-Lan had no further questions.

"It's late; I have to go home now," she said picking up her books. The next Sunday Mei-Lan was not in church and I was relieved. It bothered me to think that she had come because she thought it would please me to see her there.

I ate dinner downtown and was just putting the Honda away when I heard the phone ringing. Anneke sometimes called on Sunday but generally late in the evening. She had, as I had predicted, decided not to return to Ho-Ping. Kurt was very much better and it seemed only right for her to stay on in Germany. This time the call was not from Anneke but from Vincent Grogan in Taipei. Vincent had been faithful to his promise to keep in touch. He called every month or so, encouraging me to come to Taipei for a little R&R. But I rarely had a weekend free and when I did I was too tired to make the trip.

"Listen, Les," he said after we had finished our usual questions and answers, "I'm going to be in Chi-Yi on business this Tuesday. Can you be free by late afternoon? I'm coming down by train and I'll get a taxi out to Ho-Ping and then we can see about dinner. How about it?"

Wonderful! I could easily be free by four o'clock. See him then! I spent Monday fantasizing what conversation would be like with a native English speaker: no need to speak slowly, to enunciate every syllable; no worry about slipping into slang or working out explanations for new words or phrases. Just talking. Freely. How long had it been since I had been able to do that?

On Tuesday, contrary to my usual routine, I was out of my classroom seconds after the dismissal bell rang and down the stairs to the main entrance. Vincent was waiting for me just inside the door. He looked taller than I remembered and much fairer. A very real American. I reached out instinctively to give him a compatriotic hug but I was caught up short by his extended hand. "Many eyes watching," he said as we shook hands.

"Not bad," he nodded, as I opened the door of my apartment. "Better than you would have done in Taipei."

"It's huge," I said, "now that I have it all to myself. I'm almost embarrassed when I hear how most of my students live."

"What about the girl you lived with? She decided not to come back?"

"She needed to be home. Her fiancé was in a terrible motorcycle accident, I think I told you that. Anyway, she went back to Germany to be with him. They're going to be married this summer."

Vincent was looking around approvingly at our little stove and refrigerator. "Must be hard on you, Les. Are you the only Westerner here now?"

"The only English speaker. There's a teacher from the Philippines who speaks Spanish but that's not much help."

"I have to hand it to you for sticking it out. I must tell you, Tom never thought you would. This kind of isolation isn't easy to handle."

"It's not as bad as I would have expected. Anyhow, I'm always so busy I don't have time to notice it much. And then I've gotten quite friendly with one of my students from my fifth year English class. Li Mei-Lan."

Vincent smiled. "Mei-Lan–beautiful orchid. You have to hand it to the Chinese for names."

"And she is beautiful, too. Too bad you can't meet her; I think you'd enjoy her. Are you sure you can't stay over tonight and get a train back in the morning?"

"Afraid not this time but I haven't explained why I'm here. I came to begin negotiations for a couple of us to come to Chi-Yi permanently. We hope to do some work with the men in the factories and there's a parish that's been without a priest for months now. We're hoping to find a house on the outskirts of the city."

My heart leaped at the thought. How different it would be to have some Americans within talking distance. "When do you think you'll be coming?"

"The plan is that I'll come down in a week or so to look for a house. We've discovered that if you're not on the spot it's pretty hopeless to find a place. This afternoon I went to visit a family in the parish and they're happy to put me up while I'm house-hunting."

We had come into town for dinner and now Vincent looked at his watch. "I'd like to get the nine o'clock train if I can. The next one doesn't leave until eleven. Suppose we take a taxi to the station and then you can go on to Ho-Ping."

I rode back to Ho-Ping in a state of euphoria, waving at the old gateman who was just about to lock up as the taxi drove in. Soon Vince and a couple of other American priests were to going to be living at Chi-Yi. I would have someone to laugh with, someone to share stories with, someone to share my frustration with. Yes, of course I had been lonely but I hadn't realized how lonely until this evening. This was going to be wonderful. This was going to change my life.

By the time Vincent arrived in Chi-Yi I was able to slow my pace in school. Since it was the final semester for my students their achievements were pretty well in place and their futures decided. No last minute cramming would make very much difference. The English play was over too. It had been performed before an admiring Chinese audience most of whom, I suspected, understood very little of the dialogue. But the girls looked charming, if a bit startling in their elaborate eighteenth century English dress, their hair piled in unaccustomed ringlets and waves and their speech giving Jane Austin's words a flavor she could not have imagined.

The first weekend that Vincent was in Chi-Yi he celebrated the early morning Mass at the parish church. I waited for him outside the sacristy and as we walked down the aisle I spotted Mei-Lan sitting near the door watching us appraisingly. I beckoned to her and she followed us out onto the steps.

"This," I said to Vincent, "is Li Mei-Lan, one of my students. She will be graduating from Ho-Ping in July."

Mei-Lan bowed and Vincent, acknowledging the introduction, said, "I understand you are one of Miss Spendler's best students."

Mei-Lan lowered her head and I thought she was going to treat us to one of her humble protestations but instead she said nothing.

"Let's walk over here out of the sun," I suggested, trying to get us over an awkward moment. "Now if we were in the United States, do you know what we'd do?"

Mei-Lan shook her head.

"We'd all go out to brunch."

"Bunch?" Mei-lan asked. Clearly it was a new word.

"Brunch," Vincent enunciated slowly, "a combination of breakfast and lunch."

Mei-Lan still looked puzzled. "Only one meal?" she asked.

Vincent laughed. "Not very Chinese, right Mei-Lan?" and then added something in Mandarin.

At once her shyness vanished and she met Vincent's eyes and laughed.

"What was that all about?" I asked.

"A joke about how the Chinese like to eat," Mei-Lan explained. She was still smiling.

We walked Mei-Lan over to the bicycle racks and waved her off.

"I was going to ask her to come and have coffee with us but I wasn't sure she'd be comfortable."

"Tell me more about Mei-Lan," he asked, as I boiled the water for coffee.

"Well, as I told you, she's a fifth year student in the English division. She's bright, industrious, ambitious."

"Ah, aren't they all!" Vincent said laughing. "It must be

more than that for you to take such a shine to her."

"The first time I noticed her I had been here just a couple of weeks. I was getting frustrated unto death at all the unthinking regurgitation of what I had just said. I couldn't get an idea or an opinion out of them no matter what I did. I was just about ready to pack my bags and go home. Then one afternoon as I was correcting papers, I came to Mei-Lan's. And there, phrased in relatively correct English, was a real live opinion–something that actually differed from my presentation. It was a little breath of hope. Mei-Lan made my efforts seem worthwhile.

"Then after Anneke left she was very attentive and thoughtful . . . . She seemed to have a sixth sense about when I needed her. I think you'll enjoy Mei-Lan, Vince."

"I know: bright, industrious, ambitious." He laughed as he put down his cup. "I better get going," he said as he looked at his watch.

A good portion of my free time the following week was spent with Vincent, searching for suitable housing. It turned out to be more difficult than he had anticipated. Neither of us knew the surrounding locale and the few leads Vincent had were generally snatched up by the time we found them. We bumped along the narrow dusty streets, I clinging firmly to Vincent's waist, for although I had overcome my initial terror I still found motorcycle travel a precarious business.

"Why don't we ask Mei-Lan to go with us the next time," I asked as we sat in my apartment after a hot and fruitless search. "After all she's lived here all her life. She probably knows all those little alleyways like the palm of her hand."

Vincent shrugged. "I don't know. You don't think she'd find it an imposition?"

"Mei-Lan? She'd be thrilled. She loves to do things that make her special."

And so Mei-Lan became Vincent's real estate guide. From the beginning it was clear that three was a bad number. Mei-Lan immediately negated the idea of taking the bus. It simply did not go to the right places, she pointed out.

"We can ride three on motorcycle; I don't care," she offered.

"Not on my motorcycle." Vincent was firm.

"Everybody goes three; sometimes with little kids, four and five," Mei-Lan insisted.

But Vincent was adamant.

"I do it lots of times with my brothers," Mei-Lan protested, but Vincent shook his head.

"Look, you two go ahead. You don't need me," I finally said. "It's better to have just two anyway. I'll stay home and finish my papers."

Thus began the late afternoon explorations of Vincent and Mei-Lan. Within two weeks they had found a suitable place conveniently situated just outside the city. The house was sufficiently large and spaced so that there was at least minimal privacy.

The following evening I arranged a little celebration for the three of us. Along with the usual dumplings I had found a tin of paté and some cheese and pretzels (age indeterminate) in the International Grocery Emporium and Vincent brought along some Taiwanese beer.

Toward the end of the evening Vincent raised his glass. "I propose a toast," he said.

"Wait a minute," I cautioned. "Mei-Lan, do you know what a toast is?"

She looked uncertain and Vincent translated for her.

She looked up at him laughing. "To drink to very special person."

"Right," said Vincent. "Tonight Mei-Lan is a very special person. She has succeeded where we would have failed. Here's to Mei-Lan!"

We drank our toast and Vincent looked at his watch. "I better get back to the Changs," he said. "They go to bed early."

"What about you, Mei-Lan? Do you have your brothers' motorcycle?" I asked.

"She came over with me," Vincent explained.

"I take bus home," Mei-Lan offered.

"Certainly not. I'm taking you home. I don't want a beautiful girl walking alone around Chi-Yi at night." Beer had made Vincent expansive.

I watched them out the window: Vincent revving up his new motorcycle and Mei-Lan climbing up behind him, reaching forward to hold on to his waist as they rounded the circle and drove out toward the entrance.

The next week Fathers Paul and Steven came down from Taipei to initiate the new community and the following

Saturday night they opened their doors for a housewarming. They had invited some of the families who had helped Vincent get settled, some of the catechists from the neighboring parish, a group of Maryknollers who worked in the area–and Mei-Lan.

For the first time since I had known her Mei-Lan wore a chipa–that classic Chinese dress with its high, stiff Mandarin collar and its long side-slits. It was of printed silk, golden honey in color, and it fitted Mei-Lan's fine-boned body perfectly. Her hair looked almost lacquered, pulled back tight from her face and fashioned in an intricate knot at the back of her neck. She stood out with a kind of elegance against the plain furnishings of the house, against the men in their short-sleeved white shirts and the women in their simple print dresses.

Vincent was almost naive in his overt pleasure at introducing her, explaining how much she had helped them in finding the house and furnishing it, describing their hot dusty rides on his motorcycle, and Mei-Lan's uncanny ability to bargain. After the first few minutes of ritual shyness Mei-Lan hit her stride and as the evening progressed it was clear that if there was a shy outsider it was I.

Since most of the guests were Chinese or Taiwanese, Mandarin was the language of the evening. The priests–even Vincent, though he was the least proficient–held their own. I, however, could catch only a word here and there and I was totally unable to answer the comments addressed to me. Mei-Lan, quick to realize my difficulty, became my interpreter, staying at my side, leading me from group to group, introducing me, explaining our relationship, praising all I had done for Ho-Ping. It was a strange and sudden reversal of roles and while I knew I should be grateful, in fact her efforts only made me feel more alien.

When I saw Vincent beckoning to her from the doorway I felt relieved. Father Paul seeing me alone came over, wiping his forehead. He was the oldest of the priests, a veteran of the Shanghai mission which had been destroyed during the Communist takeover. Vincent had told me that he had tried twice to return to the Mainland but without success.

"Who needs warm beer on a night like this," he said, putting his glass on a window sill. "I gather you haven't picked up much Chinese yet," he remarked. "It's a tough language; I've been at it for years and now I have to start all over again with Taiwanese."

"I've started to study once or twice but generally I'm too busy teaching Eng-rish. Usually it doesn't bother me. We aren't permitted to use Chinese in school and I haven't had too many social opportunities."

"Lonely?" he asked.

"Oh, a little, but nowhere near as much as I would have predicted. First semester I lived with another Western teacher. We were about the same age so that made it nice. Of course, it's wonderful having Vincent here. Having a normal English conversation makes all the difference."

"For him, too, I'm sure. He was a little nervous about coming down alone. We have to thank you for all you did. Vincent said you were invaluable."

I laughed. "Hardly that. The most invaluable thing I did was introduce him to Mei-Lan."

Paul nodded, looking over at Vincent and Mei-Lan. Mei-Lan an image of oriental grace in her elegant chipa; Vincent the quintessential American–tall, thin, his hair bleached golden. They were standing in the doorway, perfectly framed, Vincent with his hands in his pockets; Mei-Lan facing him with a wine glass held up in both hands, almost like a libation.

"Mei-Lan." said Paul. "Beautiful orchid. That's certainly the truth. And here I was picturing poor old Vincent riding around on his motorcycle with some fat little Chinese mama holding on from behind." He laughed. "I shouldn't have been so sympathetic."

He tried to stifle a yawn. "Sorry, but it's early times tomorrow. I have to go back to Taipei to finish a little business and Steven and Vincent will be heading into the mountains. We're hoping to get permission to work with some of the native tribes there. They have a couple of trained catechists but no priest on a regular basis."

The guests had begun to leave and Paul excused himself, joining Vincent and Steven at the door, thanking them for coming, hoping to see them soon again, saying goodnight. Soon only Mei-Lan was left.

"Let's see if we can clean up the kitchen before we go," I suggested, but Mei-Lan hesitated.

"I told her I'd take her home," Vincent explained. "I don't like her walking around alone so late at night"

"You didn't ride your bicycle?" I was surprised. Mei-Lan never walked anywhere.

Mei-Lan giggled, looking down at her dress. "Very difficult with chipa."

CHAPTER X

"Les, why don't you wait till I come back and I can ride you home on my motorcycle," Vincent suggested.

But I shook my head. "Paul can get a taxi for me; I'll be home in no time. There's no point in your coming all the way out to Ho-Ping. You and Steven have to get an early start in the morning."

Suddenly I was out of sorts. The damp night air weighed down on me and I felt anxious and depressed. We all walked out to the main street together, Vincent shepherding Mei-Lan along the narrow alley while Paul and Steven and I walked behind.

"How come I never get to baptize any beautiful Chinese maidens?" Steven sighed. "All my converts are fifty plus."

Paul laughed. "Safer that way; don't look for trouble."

They waited with me until they flagged down a taxi and then waved me off as the driver made a precarious U-turn and started back for Ho-Ping.

XI

The next week was an unbroken round of class and class preparation. I didn't hear from Vincent and except for her presence in class I didn't see Mei-Lan. The days seemed insufferably long and dull and I began to realize how much I had enjoyed my small part in house hunting and furnishing. When Vincent called on Saturday evening I was half-asleep over a book–drugged with heat and boredom.

"Don't tell me you're asleep at nine o'clock!"

"Not asleep exactly . . . ." My voice was scratchy and I cleared my throat. "Just bored, I guess. It's been a dreary week and the heat hasn't helped. I'm full of sweat as soon as I get out of bed in the morning."

"Terrible, I know, but let me offer you the perfect solution. How about a trip up to Teh-Chi?"

"What's that?"

"A little town in the mountains by a beautiful river."

I sighed. "Sounds wonderful but I'll have to turn it down. I have early morning classes on Monday."

"No problem. We can easily do it in a day. I have the early Mass in the parish tomorrow and we can leave right after that. We should be there by noon. I have to deliver some things to the church and make arrangements for the rest of the summer but that shouldn't take long. We can easily be home before dark."

CHAPTER XI

"But are you sure we can get a bus back? I understand they go up the mountain only once a day."

"Oh, we won't be taking the bus; we'll be driving."

My heart sank. "Oh, Vincent, you don't expect me to go up through the mountains on your motorcycle. Honest, I just couldn't do it. I'd be dead of fright on the first turn." I felt angry and disappointed. Why hadn't I realized at the beginning that we would have to use his motorcycle?

"Who said motorcycle? We have a little van at our disposal for the day. The bishop offered it to us so we could transport the stuff for the church. So, how about it? Will you come?"

"I'd love to but are you sure it isn't too much for one day?"

"No problem, I promise. I'll have you back in plenty of time for a good night's sleep."

"In that case . . . ."

"Great. I'll meet you in church tomorrow and we can leave from there." There was a little pause and then Vincent said, "Les, suppose I ask Mei-Lan? She doesn't have a chance for much fun. That step-mother of hers really keeps her working. I feel sorry for the poor kid."

My reaction was so immediate that it startled me. "I don't know why you should. She doesn't have it any worse than anybody else."

As soon as it was out, I was embarrassed. Not simply for saying it but even for thinking it. "Oh, Vince, I'm sorry. What a rotten thing to say. I guess it's just an end of term reaction. Too many students, too many papers. Would you mind if we left Mei-Lan out this time?"

For a moment Vincent said nothing. He was clearly trying to grope his way past my surprising response. Finally he said, "I didn't mean to push. I just thought . . . ." He left the sentence unended. The silence was heavy but neither of us made an effort to relieve it.

The main road north from Chi-Yi toward Taichung was wide and relatively uncrowded. There were always the overcrowded lorries weaving unsteadily between lanes but once out of the city the traffic was minimal. It was only mid-morning when we approached Taichung. Here the road narrowed and there was no way around the congestion. The Sunday markets were in full sway and we stopped and started, jerked and swayed in an effort to avoid children on foot, on bicycles, strapped to their parents' backs. Finally, in desperation Vincent found a little street where we could park.

"Come on," he said, "Let's get out and get something to drink. I need to be fortified before I take on the rest of this city." Vincent's khaki shirt was soaking wet and my own skirt was stuck tight to my legs. I hadn't reckoned on a long ride without air conditioning.

We bought two Cokes–the only bottled drink we could find–and stood under a little piece of awning drinking them while the owner of the awning did his best to sell us another couple of bottles.

Vincent stuck his bottle on the ground. "OK. Ready to get on with it?"

I nodded. "You promised me a cool day in the mountains, remember?"

CHAPTER XI

"And that you will have, I promise. Just have faith."

Within the hour he had justified himself. As we climbed, the air poured in blessedly cool. But just as I had begun to lean back, resting my head against the headrest to enjoy the dramatic change in atmosphere, something else began to change. As we moved eastward, the wide level road that had led into Taichung was narrowed to two lanes, as it spiraled into the mountains, twisting and turning with no adequate banking for the narrow curves.

I closed my eyes as we slid and lurched around a particularly dangerous curve.

"Are you all right?" Vincent asked, reaching out and putting a hand on my knee.

I nodded, swallowing hard. "And I'll be even better if you keep both hands on the steering wheel."

"But you have to admit it's beautiful," he said. It was, of course, beautiful, mysteriously beautiful in the gray light of a sudden misty rain.

"Shangri-La," I said as I turned to see the soft outlines of peaks rising on both sides. There was something mystical and welcoming in the half-light, the mountains less jagged and awesome than they had appeared in full sunlight.

But by the time we arrived at Teh-Chi Dam the sun was out again in full blaze. Before we reached the town, Vincent pulled off the road onto a kind of overlook. At first I could see nothing but as we got out of the car I saw a flight of steps leading down alongside a ravine.

"There's a little refreshment area and a WC on the next landing," Vincent explained, "and at the bottom is a large youth hostel where they can accommodate a couple of hundred students during the summer vacation. Not grand luxe but neat and clean and marvelously inexpensive. I thought we might stop and get some lunch here."

The refreshment area was a small slab of concrete, meagerly covered by a sagging piece of canvas but the view compensated for everything: directly below ran the Tachia river, a cool, milky, jade-green ribbon, channeled between jagged cliffs, spare slabs of gray granite at their base but then flourishing into thick green forests as they rose. We were too high to hear even the lapping of the waters and there was no other sound, not even birds. It was a stillness so perfect that I thought even my breath might disturb it. We ate our lunch there, not talking, unwrapping our sandwiches carefully so as not to disturb the flawless silence.

"Sorry to do this, Les," Vincent said, standing up, but I think we better get on up to the church. I have a feeling it's going to rain again and I'd just as soon be out of the mountains before we hit a real storm."

"How far is the church?"

"Only about fifteen minutes."

"Do you have to come back this way?"

"Sure, it's the only road."

"Would you mind if I stayed and you picked me up on the way back?"

For a minute he looked surprised and then, "Sure. That's fine. I'll be back in an hour. You won't mind being alone?"

CHAPTER XI

I shook my head. "I need the silence a little while longer."

"OK. Suppose we say I'll pick you up on the road at three o'clock. That'll give me a little more than an hour."

But long before three o'clock the rains began, soft at first and then in a torrential downpour. Soon I could no longer see the river and even the mountains had become vague shadows. The canvas that had protected me from the sun began to flap and rip and I decided I would be better off up the steps and closer to the road. By the time Vincent returned, the torrents of rain had changed to a steady gray downpour with gusts of wind that blew the rain in horizontal sheets.

Vincent opened the passenger door. "God, Les, I'm sorry. I got back as soon as I could. Are you OK?"

"Wet but cool," I assured him, "even a little shivery."

"Here, do you want my jacket?"

I shook my head. Being cool, I assured him, was an unsurpassable delight. "Do you think we should wait here until it stops?" I asked, as the car skidded across the shale and onto the main road.

"It might be a long wait. I'd just as soon get back to Taichung before dark. It'll be OK; don't worry. At least we don't have to worry about traffic."

For the next half hour we didn't talk, Vincent leaning forward, focusing all his attention on the road. As we approached the first of several tunnels he slowed down.

"Damn, I always forget they never have any lights in their tunnels and I'm not sure where the headlights are in this car; I've never driven it before. Maybe I can make it without lights. Thank God, nobody's coming in the other direction. He edged forward slowly and then stopped.

"Leslie, look in the glove compartment; maybe there's a flashlight."

But just as I was opening the latch and fumbling inside, I was jolted back against the headrest and then deafened by a series of bone-rattling detonations. There in the tunnel it seemed that the world was lifting up only to come down in small pieces on my head. When, finally, the thunder stopped and I opened my eyes, I found myself in pitch blackness. Next to me Vincent moved, reaching out and putting his arm around me.

"My God, Les, are you all right?"

I couldn't answer, I could only cling to him, my ears ringing and echoing with the reverberation.

After a few minutes he eased away from me and I could hear him fumbling with the door handle. I wanted to tell him to stay, not to leave me alone in this terrifying dark, but I had no voice. I heard his footsteps circling the car and then he was back again.

"We're lucky to be alive. There's been a cave-in at the far end of the tunnel. The entrance is completely covered. Happily we can still get out the way we came in."

Vincent groped his way over to the passenger side and helped me out. Little by little we stumbled back toward the thick gray light. When we reached the entrance we found it had stopped raining. Up the road in the direction of the hostel patches of blue were already forming but in the direction of Taichung the sky was still an ominous yellow-gray.

"Les, stay here. You can lean against the wall. I want to walk up and see just what did happen."

But I shook my head. I couldn't stay alone. I couldn't trust the wall. Without a word I took Vincent's hand and together we edged our way along the narrow strip at the side of the gorge. But we were able to go no more than a dozen yards for ahead of us the destruction was immense. More than half the tunnel had collapsed and the debris was scattered clear across the road. Giant slabs of stone and concrete completely blocked the highway.

Vincent exhaled his breath between his teeth. "So much for our trip back to Taichung. It will take them at least a day to clean up this mess."

"What'll we do?"

"Try to back the car out and turn it around and go back to the hostel. Maybe they'll let us have a room. If not, we can drive on to the little town although I'm not sure what we can find there."

Watching Vincent back the car out and then attempt to turn it on that wet narrow road with the gorge and the river thundering below was almost as terrifying as the tunnel cave-in. I stood by the side of the road, trying to guide him as he manipulated the van but I was shaking so that I could hardly control my hands. Another sudden shower caught me as I stood there and I was soaking wet by the time Vincent opened the passenger door and beckoned me over to the car.

Although the old fellow who acted as caretaker for the hostel was initially suspicious of the two sodden Westerners whose Chinese was not equal to their tale of misfortune, he eventually shrugged and showed us a small room near the entrance where we could spend the night. Except for two bedrolls at the side of the tatami floor and a single dim bulb hanging from a chain, the room was bare. Soon our host further repented and brought us into his kitchen, offering us rice and a bowl of delicious clear soup with tiny clams, still in their shells, no bigger than my thumb nail.

The food relaxed me and I was half asleep by the time we returned to our room. Our window faced away from the river and if there was turbulence during the night I never knew it. When I woke Vincent was already gone and I was grateful to find that my dress which I had spread out on the tatami mat was basically dry. It wasn't raining but the mist that swirled up from the river was so dense that it obscured everything. I started up the concrete steps leading to the road and at the top I saw Vincent waving at me.

"Breakfast," he said, waving a rice box at me. "Are you up to it?"

"Absolutely."

"Did you have a good sleep?"

"Like one dead."

"Don't joke; we almost were. Here, look what I got. Not quite Dunkin' Donuts but the Chinese equivalent, commonly known as greasy sticks."

I took one tentatively. "They're still warm."

"Straight out of the frying pan."

"Good," I nodded. "Like a cruller–sort of. And where's

my coffee?"

"That was beyond my ability but you can have your choice: tea or soy milk. The idea is to dunk your greasy stick in the soy milk."

"I pass. I'll stick to tea."

The mist was beginning to lift, replaced by a cool breeze. I looked at my watch: eight o'clock–time for me to be in my classroom.

"Vincent, I have to call Ho-Ping. I should have done it last night but I was too muddled to remember. When do you think we can get back?"

"From what they were saying in the village this morning, the road will be closed at least until tomorrow morning. And I'm afraid the telephone is out, too. The hostel has a phone and so does the headman in the village but the storm whacked out the lines and I gather that fixing them is not a priority."

"So we have all day," I said.

Vincent laughed. "Try not to sound so tragic. It might even be fun. It seems to be turning into a nice day."

"But I feel bad about not getting a message back to Ho-Ping. Do you think they'll hear about the storm and the cave-in?"

"Probably not. News travels slowly out of the mountains. Listen, Les, they'll get along without you. Why don't we just think of this as an unexpected holiday? We can drive into the village; there's even a little noodle house there. And they told me there's a path down to the river and a couple of row boats. How about it?"

It took me most of the morning to shake off the terror that still shrouded me. The slightest darkening of the sky made my heart pound; a sudden gust of wind sent me reliving the horrors of that dark tunnel. But Vincent was adamant, determined to pull me out of my disquiet and by afternoon he had succeeded. Noodles lavishly flavored with shrimp and a bottle of Chinese beer helped. By the time we had scrambled down the mountain path and dangled our feet from a rock into the clear green river, something of my sense of adventure had returned.

I had leaned back against a rock, cushioning my head with Vincent's knapsack. The sun was wonderful, warm but far from the fierce heat of the south.

I was half asleep when Vincent said, "Les, did Mei-Lan see you last week?"

"No. Just in class. Why?" In fact, I had seen less and less of Mei-Lan as the semester came to an end. I had attributed this to increased hours at her job and perhaps disappointment that she had received no positive news from colleges in America. My encouragement which for a while had buoyed her spirits had begun to turn sour. She no longer wanted to talk about her future. No doubt her failure to get a scholarship seemed like a loss of face in her eyes.

"There was something she wanted to tell you."

I sat up. "Not a scholarship? She didn't get a scholarship?" I had almost given up hope.

"No, not a scholarship. Has Mei-Lan ever talked about religion with you?"

"Not for a while. When we first talked about her going to

America, she was curious to know if all American students were Christian. I disabused her of that. She seemed to think that she would be expected to have some Western religion. Once I assured her that no one would expect that of her, I don't think she ever mentioned it again. Why?"

"Mei-Lan would like to be baptized and she has asked me to prepare her."

It was more than surprise that kept me silent. It was again that sudden uncontrollable flicker of resentment that had pricked me when Vincent had suggested bringing Mei-Lan on our outing. When, finally, I asked, "And are you going to?" my voice betrayed me. It was flat and cold and filled with something akin to disapproval.

Vincent caught it at once. He turned toward me, eyeing me quizzically. "I gather you don't think it's a good idea?"

I could find nothing to say. I hardly understood my own reaction. It was exaggerated and inappropriate and I stammered in an effort to make some rational explanation. "I guess I'm always a little worried that Mei-Lan wants too much to please."

Vincent frowned. "But why would she want to please me? I have no influence over her life. It would make more sense if she were trying to please you. You could be instrumental in promoting her; but she doesn't seem even to have told you."

I shrugged. I could find no counter argument. "Have you started instructions?"

"Yes, we've been working for a couple of weeks now. I must say, Les, that I find Mei-Lan very serious, very industrious, very devoted."

I smiled. The words were identical to those I had used when I first described Mei-Lan to Vincent. "I'm sure you do," I said. Again, that note of uncontrolled resentment.

"Do you object to that?" There was something curt in Vincent's voice that I had never heard before. "You seem to be down on Mei-Lan these days; what's the matter?"

I didn't want the day to end like this; I didn't want to spoil this beautiful place. I reached over and put my hand on his arm. "Vincent, I don't know what's the matter and that's the truth. Maybe I'm just embarrassed and disappointed that no scholarship has come through for Mei-Lan. After all, I started this thing. I put ideas in her head and now I've failed to deliver. Maybe I feel ashamed or guilty. I don't know. Anyway, I don't want to have this tangled up with her baptism. If that's what she wants I think it's wonderful. OK?"

Vincent nodded. "The other half of this is she wants you to be her godmother."

I was a little more in control now and I was sincere when I said, "I'm flattered but wouldn't it be better if she had a Chinese godmother? Somebody who'll be around to support her? After all, I'll probably be going back to the States by the end of the summer."

"Practically I suppose you're right but it would have to be the right person. Mei-Lan is very bright. I wouldn't want to put her in the hands of someone who couldn't deal with her concerns. Is there someone on the faculty who might be able?"

Madame Hsu came immediately to my mind. She was

strong, educated, with a long history of Christianity in her family. She would be far more able to understand and help Mei-Lan than I would be. She would never make it easy but that was probably just as well. The more I thought about it, the more it seemed that she would be ideal.

"Sounds great to me," Vincent said, as I explained something of Madame Hsu's background to him. "Why don't you sound her out and then if she's willing I'll talk to Mei-Lan."

He looked at his watch. "I'm going to take the car and go down to the landslide. They thought they might have the road cleared by the end of the day."

I panicked. "Vince, we're not going back down that road now, are we? It'll be dark in an hour."

He laughed. "Not even in my most adventurous youth would I try that. But if they have cleared the road we could get an early start and get back to Chi-Yi by midday. In that case I suggest an early supper at our local noodle house and an early-to-bed. We should get on the road as soon as we have some visibility."

And so the next morning while the mountains were still mist-shrouded we started back to Taichung. Neither of us spoke as we drove slowly through the remainder of the tunnel and on to the road, made more narrow now by the boulders that had still not been cleared away. The rest of the trip went surprisingly well. There were few lorries on the mountain road and even getting through Taichung was far less difficult than it had been on Sunday.

We arrived at Ho-Ping just before noon. Vincent parked the van in front of my apartment and carried my satchel and the tote which had carried our lunch upstairs.

"It wasn't quite what I had in mind," he said as we stood by the stairwell saying goodbye. "I had it planned as a day of peace and tranquility."

"Well, we had that, too. Teh-Chi was beautiful and I guess even the evil tunnel won't seem so bad in retrospect."

"Bad enough. I almost got you killed."

In the distance we heard the long shrill bell that signaled the end of morning classes. "I should get going," he said, looking at his watch. "You probably want to get a shower before your afternoon classes. Don't forget to talk to Madame Hsu, will you? That sounds like a capital idea."

We were standing on the landing and Vincent reached over and put his arms around me and kissed me lightly on the cheek. He saw the shadow before I did and pulled away from me abruptly. When I turned, I saw Mei-Lan, half-way up the stairs, looking at us appraisingly.

The embrace could not have been more innocently American–a hug, a brush against the cheek, the ordinary ritual for goodbye and thank you. But we could not have handled it more foolishly. We stood like two guilty adolescents, awkward and silent.

Mei-Lan, on the other hand, in her crisp blue uniform and her hair swept back in a French knot was perfectly in control. There was no smile when she said, "We very worry about you. Nobody know where you are. Then I call Father Paul and he say you go away with Miss Leslie."

She stood there like our mentor, as though she expected an explanation and a confession of guilt.

CHAPTER XI

Vincent had recovered a little of his poise but his voice was defensive when he answered. "Of course I didn't 'go away' with Miss Leslie. We went up to Teh-Chi where I had business and then we got caught in a storm. Didn't you have a storm down here?"

"Very nice day down here."

"Well, it was a hell of a mess in the mountains, I can tell you. We were almost killed." I wished Vincent was not so volatile.

"Very sorry. But glad you home now." She turned to me. "You have class this afternoon?"

"Of course, as soon as I get a shower." I could hear the apology in my voice and I hated it. Everything was wrong and I could find no words to make it right.

"I tell the dean; she be very happy," and Mei-Lan turned and walked down the stairs.

"God, that was stupid," Vince said when she was gone. "I never should have pulled away like that. We could probably have carried it off if I'd just had the sense to act casual. Sorry, Les. I'll have to explain some Western customs to Mei-Lan some day."

I smiled and nodded as he started down the stairs but I wasn't sure Mei-Lan was open to explanations.

XII

I didn't sleep much that night. I didn't want to. I wanted to wrestle down my sudden change of attitude toward Mei-Lan. When had my pleasure in my role of fairy-godmother shifted? I sifted through my memories: afternoons spent together talking, planning her future; the day at Tienhsiang with our trip to the Buddhist monastery; my pride in introducing her to Vincent. Happy times all. When then?

And suddenly I was faced with the image of Mei-Lan as she had been at the housewarming party. Not the earnest, docile student of my classroom but a young woman of engaging beauty, at ease, poised, almost arrogant in her charm. I saw her as she had stood at the doorway with Vincent, her golden chipa following the lines of her body, her upswept hair emphasizing the grace of her shoulders and neck. I had felt ill-at-ease that night, graceless and outmatched, and I realized now–as I had not before–that I had resented Mei-Lan.

I closed my eyes and let my mind go where it would. I had lost my place that night. I was no longer mentor or fairy-godmother, neither teacher nor leader. The role I had marked out for myself was undermined and I had no other to replace it. Mei-Lan, not I, was leading the dance and I could not keep pace with the music.

But there was more. I began to recognize it now. Twice during the weekend my resentment had flared up. Once when Vincent suggested including Mei-Lan in our trip; again when he had told me he was preparing her for baptism. My hostility was too sudden and unbidden to come from any rational source. It was as though some secret fire, burning unacknowledged, had burst through the reserves that covered it. In every case Vincent had been involved. Again that image rose up: Vincent and Mei-Lan as they had stood together at the party–fair and dark, broad-shouldered and slender, West and East.

I could feel my face flushing, sensing my shame even before I could acknowledge it. Jealousy? Was that the root? Jealous of Mei-Lan because of Vincent? But how stupid! Vincent did not belong to me. We were not lovers. Friends, yes, but in the most casual sort of way. Two people with the same background, the same language, the same basic perspective. We sought each other out because there was no one else. We took pleasure, excessive pleasure perhaps, simply in speaking together in a world where no one else would quite understand the jokes, the slang, the nuances of language that were the channels of our self-expression.

"Don't be surprised if you go a little crazy out there," a friend of Tom's had warned me before I left home. "Something happens when you're the only Westerner in a foreign land. Believe me, I know."

When I had looked at him questioningly, he only shrugged. "Hard to explain. Things get heightened–emotions, desires. I suppose it's only natural. All the ordinary channels are blocked and we grasp at what we have no right to."

Had jealousy, that vice I had always found so abhorrent, found a place in me?

I lay there for a while, listening to the clack-clack-clack of the lizards and learning to acknowledge this new truth.

By the time I heard the breakfast cooks shuffling across the courtyard I felt I had a grip on myself. I turned over for a couple of hours sleep with the firm resolution that Mei-Lan would certainly not suffer because of my stupidities. I would continue to do everything I could to get her a scholarship to America–if not for this year, then for the next. And I would present her desire for baptism to Madame Hsu in the most convincing manner possible. As for my feelings of jealousy over Mei-Lan and Vincent–that I hoped, would work itself out now that it had been brought to the clear light of day.

I had missed my calligraphy class on Monday and so it was another week before I saw Madame Hsu. It was clear from the first moment that I had not practiced. She said nothing as I struggled through the lesson but at the end as I put away my brush, she asked, "Is it your wish to continue with your calligraphy lessons?" I assured her that it was, apologizing for my negligence and explaining about my unexpected stay at Teh-Chi Dam.

It seemed to me like a good time to introduce Mei-Lan and I began. "Father Vincent told me while we were there that he was preparing Li Mei-Lan for baptism. He hopes that she will be ready during the summer."

I had expected her response to be enthusiastic. The number of converts at Chi-Yi was so few that a conversion was always a matter of celebration to the small Catholic congregation; but Madame Hsu merely nodded, saying nothing.

"As we were discussing it, I suggested that you might be willing to be Mei-Lan's godmother. It will be very important for her to have someone to support and encourage her."

CHAPTER XII

Still Madame Hsu said nothing and I found myself limping. "She is a very intelligent young woman and I'm sure she will have many questions . . . ." I paused, not sure how to elicit some response.

At last she turned to face me. "Are you sure you are acting wisely in encouraging Li Mei-Lan in this?"

"Wisely?" Her meaning escaped me.

"In the best interests of Mei-Lan?"

"I don't know what you mean. Why wouldn't it be in her best interests?"

"What does she expect from this religious act?" There was the slightest color of disdain in Madame Hsu's voice and it set up my defenses.

"What does she expect? What any convert would expect–to become a Christian, a Catholic, to be received into the Christian communion . . . ." I was tripping over the formulas meaninglessly.

"And to go to college in the United States of America."

It was not a question. It was a statement, incontestable and absolute.

Surprise–and anger–kept me silent.

"You think I am being very brutal," she continued. "Perhaps. But I hope that what I have said will lead you to reflect on what you are doing."

"What I'm doing? I'm not doing anything. The question of Mei-Lan's baptism has been entirely between Father Vincent and herself. You act as though I'm trying to coerce

Mei-Lan into becoming a Christian." The irony bit into me–that I who had worked so hard to conquer my resentment of Mei-Lan should now be marked and condemned as her advocate.

"That was not my meaning; quite the opposite. I'm not sure you have properly identified Mei-Lan's desire."

"Why are you questioning her? Is there something wrong in wanting to be a Christian?"

Again that implacable voice: "Are you sure that that is Mei-Lan's desire?"

At last I followed Madame Hsu's meaning and words that had eluded me in my first shock now came tumbling out. "What are you accusing her of? What right have you to insinuate that she is only being baptized to get to the United States? She doesn't have to be a Christian to get a scholarship in America. There's no connection."

"Perhaps not for you; but it may be very different for Mei-Lan. Li Mei-Lan is a very ambitious girl. I'm sure you've recognized that by now."

"What's wrong with that? She's bright. Her English is very good. Why shouldn't she dream of doing something fine for herself?"

Madame Hsu was looking straight at me, scrutinizing me as though she hoped to find an answer to something that escaped her.

"You know, Miss Spendler, we have worked together here for a number of months and I admire what you have been able to do at Ho-Ping. You are a fine teacher with many qualities that your students appreciate: you are kind, patient, generous but you are also a little naive, a little credulous. I have said this to you before and I say it now not to hurt you but to try to spare you from hurt."

I think she would have gone on had I let her. Now in retrospect I understand what she was trying to say. But at the time her words only confused me. When I looked at her I saw her transformed into one of those lacquered Chinese empresses–cruel and implacable–and I hated her.

I got up and reached for my box of brushes. "Thank you for your advice," I said. "I think it would be better if we terminated my lessons. I expect to be very busy for the remainder of the semester."

She made no effort to keep me. She rose and opened the door, bowing as I walked out into the blistering sunshine.

When Vincent called that evening I told him simply that Madame Hsu did not feel that she could assume this responsibility. I saw no need to say any more and happily he asked no questions.

"Well, I guess that leaves you, Les. How about it?"

"I suppose so but I worry about leaving Mei-Lan here on her own with no support. I thought godparents were supposed to foster and support."

"They are. But you're expecting Mei-Lan to get to the States sooner or later, aren't you? In which case it would be far better for her to have a godparent over there."

I had to concede he was right and I tried to dismiss my hesitation. "But, you know," I reminded him, "Mei-Lan has never mentioned this to me. Are you sure that she wants me as her godmother?"

"It will be fine. Don't worry. I'm going to see her later this week and I can talk to her about it."

When my literature class met on Friday afternoon, it was obvious that Vincent had talked with Mei-Lan. She looked at me with that barely noticeable smile that suggested a secret understanding. And when class was over she waited for me–the first time in several weeks.

"Maybe we have time to talk little bit this weekend?" she asked.

"Of course. You have to work on Saturday, don't you?"

"I start early morning so they let me finish four o'clock. I tell them I have to be home to cook for my parents."

"And do you?" I asked.

"Oh, no." Mei-Lan's smile was amused. "It makes very nice excuse. My boss likes girls who take care of their parents."

I wanted to point out that lying was not the best way of beginning her religious conversion but that ground was too murky.

"Would you like me to meet you in Chi-Yi?"

Mei-Lan hesitated. "Maybe I come to your house. More quiet."

I nodded. "Fine. I'll expect you sometime after four."

Promptly at 4:30 I heard a motorcycle pull into the courtyard and saw Mei-Lan and Vincent dismounting from his Honda. The same uncontrollable annoyance that I had fought so hard to conquer rose up inside me but this time at least it did not take me unawares.

I heard them talking on the stairs. Vincent practicing his Chinese and Mei-Lan laughing at him.

"This one mocks my every effort," Vincent said, nodding toward Mei-Lan as he followed her in the door.

"He say his horse has gray hair," Mei-Lan giggled.

"Horse, mother, whatever. How can anybody get all these tones in place?"

They sat companionably on the sofa near the window. I had put water on to boil and sat on a straight chair near the kitchen.

"Mei-Lan has some news for you," Vincent said, leaning back and smiling at Mei-Lan."

"Oh?" It was the best I could do.

"Father Vincent prepare me for baptism to be a Christian."

"Congratulations, Mei-Lan. That's wonderful news." I tried to get the proper mixture of surprise and happiness in my voice. "When will you be baptized?"

Mei-Lan looked at Vincent and he nodded encouragingly. "Maybe in summertime; before you leave Ho-Ping." She paused and Vincent nodded at her again. "I like very much if you be my godmother."

"That would be a great honor, Mei-Lan. Thank you. Are you sure you wouldn't rather have someone who lives here permanently be your godmother?"

She smiled securely. "Oh, no. Anyway when I go to

America then I find you and Father Vincent there."

That was something I had not known ahead of time and I raised my eyebrows in surprise. "Really?"

"My five years on mission will be over in a year and a half and I'll be back working in the States, at least for a while," Vincent explained.

"I didn't realize that." My voice was curt and aggrieved.

"I guess it just never came up. Mei-Lan was asking me how long I'd be in Taiwan, so I told her."

I could hear the water begin to boil. "Excuse me," I said. "Would you both like coffee?"

"I suspect Mei-Lan would prefer tea, wouldn't you Mei-Lan?" Vincent asked.

I felt suddenly demoted from hostess to servant, relegated to menial tasks. The stupidity of my own reactions infuriated me. I seemed to be turning into a weathervane: defending Mei-Lan in front of Madame Hsu and now turning upon her as though she were my adversary.

When Mei-Lan reached out to take her tea, I noticed a narrow silver ring with a small jade stone on her right hand.

"That's a lovely ring, Mei-Lan; I never noticed it before."

Her happiness was patent. "Father Vincent buy for me."

No answer could have been less expected and my shock was obvious.

"Hold on, Mei-Lan!" Vincent was clearly jolted by Mei-Lan's explanation. "When we finished doing all the shopping for the house," he explained, "we all wanted to give Mei-Lan a present to thank her for all she did for us. Mei-Lan said she had always wanted a ring so the two of us went shopping and this is what Mei-Lan picked out."

But Vincent's explanation did nothing to diminish Mei-Lan's pride. She fingered the ring, turning it and holding it up to be admired.

"It's very beautiful, Mei-Lan. The jade is a lovely shade. Is it Taiwanese jade?"

She nodded, rubbing her finger against the stone. "Jade is for happiness," she said.

We talked for a little while more. Mei-Lan had grown much more articulate in the last few months and she talked freely about some of the conditions on the Island, the state of education, the difficulty of getting into the universities.

"Well, please God, Mei-Lan, I hope this time next year you'll be heading for a university in the United States. I know Miss Leslie is doing everything she can. These things take time. Whoops!" He looked at his watch. "I better get you home."

But Mei-Lan shook her head. "I leave bicycle here yesterday so now I can ride home." Clearly Mei-Lan had no intention of arriving home on the back of Vincent's Honda.

I saw nothing of Vincent for the next two weeks. I waited for him on Sunday after the early Mass and we walked back together to my apartment for coffee. "How is Mei-Lan doing?" I asked as we waited for the water to boil.

Vincent was leafing through the *China Post* and didn't immediately answer. When he did, it was absently, as though the paper absorbed him completely. "She's OK."

I waited for something else to follow and when it didn't I said, "Is that all you're going to say about my prospective godchild?"

"My God, Leslie, what do you want me to say? That she's the Little Flower of China?" The reply was so unexpected and so cutting that I was stunned.

He put down the paper and stood up. "Sorry, Les, that was completely out of line. The heat must be getting me. We all seem to be on edge these days. It's typhoon season; that probably accounts for some of it. In fact, I need to talk to you about Mei-Lan. I have to go up to the mountains this morning. We're having a big celebration–Mass, baptisms, weddings, the works. Maybe I'll stop in when I get back if it's not too late. If not, I'll drop in Monday afternoon."

That Sunday afternoon stretched endlessly. For once I had no school work to do but I was too tired and hot to think of doing anything else. I lay on my bamboo mat, my body wet with perspiration, my hair sticky and damp against my neck. By evening a little breeze had picked up and I thought of taking the Honda and going down to the dumpling house for supper. But just as I was backing the bike out of the hallway, one of the resident students came toward me, waving a message: a typhoon was bearing down on us from the Philippines where it had already done serious damage. Everyone was to stay indoors with the windows closed. The building was very strong, she assured me, and I should not be afraid.

Before I could ask her anything else, she was running

across the courtyard to deliver further warnings. For the next five hours I sat waiting for the Tai-Fung–the Great Wind–but although the air grew dark and heavy nothing stirred. Even the slight evening breeze had died down and there was an ominous quiet over everything. I wondered if the typhoon had changed its course after all. About eleven o'clock I took a shower and went to bed. The heat was sweltering and although the message had been to keep all windows closed, I could not imagine living closed up for the rest of the night and I opened my two large windows as far as they would go.

I had been asleep only about an hour when the Great Wind struck. In the few seconds before I could get to the windows, everything on my desk was blown off, my book case was toppled and my two wall hangings ripped from their brackets. The rain poured over me in torrents as I tugged to close the windows. The electricity was already off and I groped along the kitchen shelves to find a candle and some matches. But even with everything battened down, the candle spluttered and wavered. Its erratic dance made me more nervous than the darkness and I finally blew it out. For the rest of the night I sat on my bed, my back braced against the wall, wet with sweat. At first I had pushed aside my mosquito net, thinking I might get a little more air without it but it was soon evident that the typhoon had done nothing to quiet the predatory tastes of the mosquitoes.

Even with the coming of daylight the storm did not abate. The wind crashed and roared and I wondered what was happening to those frail shacks along the river and in the poorer quarters of the town. After a while I stood up and wandered around in the half-light. I wasn't frightened for my physical safety; it seemed quite true that our substantial buildings could easily withstand a typhoon and we were too far inland to worry about a tidal wave. That would be the terror of the coastal cities. Even so, my body jangled. Part of it was from the noise, part from the unrelieved heat.

I was dying for a cup of coffee but I had no way to make hot water. I tried to use the thermos of boiling water I had filled the night before, but it had cooled considerably and the drink I made was too bitter to swallow. As I threw it out, I realized that I must be careful to conserve drinking water since I would have no way of boiling water until the storm was over and power restored. I poured a few ounces of water into a cup and slowly licked it up, drop by drop, washing it about in my mouth before swallowing it.

What increased my nervousness was the fact that my windows were frosted–for reasons neither Anneke nor I could ever figure out–and with them closed I was left with no visibility. At one point, about noon, it seemed to me that the wind had abated and I went over to raise the window enough to let me see out. But just as I did, the gusts increased and I saw a large section of the walkway roof sailing past my window. Another gust came straight at me and, soaking wet, I was flung away from the window. I knew I had to get the window closed and I crawled back toward it, reaching up and pulling it down with all my strength. The floor was slippery with rain but I was too hot and exhausted to do anything about it.

By mid-afternoon the wind did, in fact, abate, and by evening we were left with only intermittent rain. I put on a pair of jeans and a T-shirt and ventured out. The sky was still leaden but everything was quiet. The walkway between the buildings had disappeared completely. The playing field was a morass and every piece of vegetation was flattened into the muddy ground.

The typhoon was over but my final week in Taiwan is forever linked with those twenty-four defenseless hours of furious storm. The typhoon was like a symbolic atmosphere, savaging everything in its sudden fury and isolating me in an eerie half-light.

XIII

With typical Chinese resilience school resumed within twenty-four hours. Damage to the classrooms was surprisingly small. The fact that much of the area was open space was to our advantage for there was a minimum of broken windows. Teachers and students slogged through the mud in great good humor, eating cold lunches in a dark cafeteria and waiting patiently for electricity to be restored.

Vincent did not return to Chi-Yi until Thursday. Happily he had escaped the full force of the storm which had not moved north as predicted but veered east into the South China Sea. The telephone lines were still out but he sent me a note with a student who lived in his area asking me to have breakfast with him after Mass on Sunday.

He brought a jar of instant coffee that his sister had sent him and a large thermos of boiling water from their house where the electricity had been restored and we sat in my apartment luxuriating. It was my first hot coffee in a week and it tasted wonderful. I had been eating in the cafeteria since the typhoon. I hadn't had the courage to brave the sodden roads with their deep puddles and potholes in order to store up on food.

"Sorry," I apologized, as we sat nibbling some dry little cakes. "I haven't been able to manage anything else."

"No problem." Vincent had put his cup down on the table and was standing looking out the window. "You had a worse time of it here than we did up in the mountains."

"So you said."

"We were lucky. There's so little protection up there; it could have been devastating."

The conversation rambled on with Vincent moving about restlessly. "God, it's hot in here, Les; don't you have a fan?" he asked as he wiped the back of his hand against his forehead.

"No electricity, remember?"

He nodded absently. He sat down again, leaning forward, his elbows on his knees. The silence was oppressive. I told myself he was just tired, worn out from the anxiety of the trip but it seemed more than that. I wondered if something had happened up in the mountains that he wasn't able to talk about. I got up and went into the kitchen to make more coffee, using the last of the boiling water Vincent had brought. When I came out, Vincent looked straight at me for the first time.

"Les, I have to talk to you about Mei-Lan; I saw her again this week for quite a long period." He was bent over again, his hands between his knees. I waited. It seemed a long time before he went on. "I don't think I can baptize Mei-Lan, at least not now."

Whatever I had expected, it was not that.

Again I waited. But this time Vincent said nothing.

"What happened?" I finally asked.

He had gotten up again and was standing by the window. "The thing is, Les," he said turning toward me, "nothing happened. We go on with catechism, with question and explanation and she's letter-perfect. I can't fault her on a thing."

"But . . . ?"

"That's it. I'm not sure what the 'but' is. I have a feeling that when I'm with her, she's straining to pass a test, to pass it very well because if she does, I will be pleased and reward her."

"And baptism will be her reward?"

Vincent sighed and nodded his head. "I guess so. I don't really know. I've never dealt with anything like this before. Maybe I'm all off track. But I know I can't baptize anyone unless I feel there is some whole-hearted commitment to what she's doing."

"And you don't think there is with Mei-Lan?"

He sighed again. "So help me, I don't. I can't put my finger on anything specific but when I'm with her I feel as though she's using the whole process for some other end. God, it's murky, isn't it?" he said, wiping his forehead again. "And the thing is, of course, that I could be totally wrong. I feel as though I'm called on to make a judgment without understanding the evidence."

As he spoke I was recalling my conversation with Madame Hsu. I had never told Vincent what had actually happened beyond her refusal to be Mei-Lan's godmother. Now I wondered if perhaps it might help him, for she had said in far blunter terms some of what Vincent was trying to sort out.

When I told him he looked amazed. "Some lady, Madame Hsu. I didn't think the Chinese would be so forthright about their own." He leaned back and closed his eyes for a minute. "Maybe she's right. I know something's off-track, even though I can't pin it down."

"What are you going to tell Mei-Lan?"

"That's the question of the year, isn't it?"

"Can't you simply suggest that she needs more instruction, more time to grow into the spirit of Christianity?"

He nodded. "Sure, I can do that. I just don't want to make a promise that won't work out. That's not fair to her."

"But maybe it will work out. You have to give her that possibility, don't you?"

"I do, of course."

"But you don't believe in it, is that it?"

"Les, all I can tell you is that something is wrong. God help me, I wish I could get a hold on it but so far I can't."

"When are you going to see Mei-Lan?"

"She's coming over this evening. Paul and Steven are both going to be out so we'll have a little privacy. No matter what I say it's going to be tough. I know she's told her friends about her baptism so of course having it delayed will be a loss of face."

We stood and I walked down the stairs with him and waited while he unlocked his Honda. "I'll give you a call this evening after I see Mei-Lan," he said as he started up his machine.

I shook my head. "You can't; no telephone."

"OK, tomorrow then," he called as he turned onto the

driveway.

That evening I was just coming out of the shower after an unsuccessful effort to wash my hair in cold water when I thought I heard someone on the stairs. A minute later there was a light knock. As I wrapped a towel around my head, I looked over at the clock. It was after eleven. No student would ever come to see me at this hour. The knock came again and then Vincent's voice.

"Les, it's me. Will you open the door, please. I've got to talk to you."

God, I thought, it's Mei-Lan. She's kicked up a real tempest. I opened the door and Vincent came in without a word. It was still stiflingly hot and I started to open the blinds so we'd get more air. But Vincent reached out to stop me. "Please don't, Les. I don't want anyone to see me here."

"The guard must have seen you come in."

"No, I don't think so. I didn't come over on my Honda. I walked."

To walk would have taken him over an hour. I looked at him in amazement and as I did I realized that whatever had taken place between him and Mei-Lan had been far more ruinous than anything I had imagined.

He sat in a chair by the window and I gave him a glass of tepid water. It was all I had. He drank it slowly and then put the glass down on the table, very carefully, like a man not sure of his control. He looked up at me and I thought he was going to say something but nothing came. When finally he did speak it was not looking at me but staring across the room at a Chinese scroll of a Buddhist monk standing alone on a high cliff.

"Mei-Lan expects me to marry her."

My heart leaped and the room shifted; I shook my head trying to set it right. "But, Vincent, that's ridiculous."

His lips were pressed together almost in a smile. "Ridiculous, indeed, but true, I'm afraid."

"But Vincent, she can't imagine . . . ."

"Ah, but she can and she does, my dear Leslie."

"But how could she? She knows you're a priest and that you can't marry."

"Does she? I'm not sure she does. After all, as she pointed out very clearly, there is Father Webley who is married with three children."

"But he's not a Roman Catholic; he's Episcopalian."

"I fear these are subtle distinctions to which Mei-Lan and most other Chinese are not yet party. For them it all goes under the umbrella of Christianity."

"But even so, why would Mei-Lan ever think . . . ." I was trying to be rational in a wholly irrational situation.

"Why indeed. But I assure you she gave me some very good reasons. It seems that Mei-Lan and I have 'gone out' together, that we have shared meals together, that I invited her to a party and introduced her to my friends and that–and this, of course, is the clincher–I bought her a ring."

"But you didn't buy her the ring. You all wanted to give her something to thank her for all she had done for you.

She was the one who chose a ring."

"And I was the one who bought it for her. I should have bought it when she wasn't with me. I should have brought it home and had all three of us give it to her. Maybe I shouldn't have bought it for her at all. But the fact is I did and I gave it to her, there in the store, in public, as she was quick to point out."

He held out his glass and I went out to get more water. "Les, tell me," he said, as I put the glass down, "did you have some inkling of this?"

I shook my head. He was looking at me quizzically. "There were a couple of times when you seemed so down on Mei-Lan; I wondered if you were on to something I was missing."

"Not this. Ambition maybe. The kind of thing Madame Hsu pointed out–but not this." The consequences of what Vincent was telling me were just beginning to penetrate. "What are you going to do?"

He shrugged. "I haven't had much time to think about it. I'll have to tell Paul and Stephen, of course. I imagine they'll suggest that I go away for a while, maybe back to Taipei or maybe even the States. I'm due for a little R&R. Les, I want you to know I've never done anything–anything–that would indicate to Mei-Lan that I was in love with her. God help me, it never even occurred to me."

"Is that what she says, that you led her to believe that you were in love with her?"

"Well, she thinks I intended to marry her, so what's the difference? My God, inviting her to a house-warming party, taking her home a couple of times. What could be more innocent?"

What, indeed, but then I remembered Ruby Gao. Ruby Gao who had lost her job and her reputation for what was equally innocent.

"God, Les, it was terrible. She stood there in front of me saying all these unimaginable things. I think it wouldn't have been so awful if she'd had on her chipa and had her hair up the way she did at the house-warming but there she was in her school uniform–all white and blue and innocent–with her hair in a braid down her back, looking about fourteen."

He put his hands over his face and his shoulders were shaking. When he looked up the pain in his eyes made me turn away. "Yet she was so damn implacable, Les. No tears, no tempest, just a terrible kind of rage. What is that line about jealousy being hard as hell? It was like that–hard as hell. She says that I have destroyed her, that everyone will say she's a bad element, that she will never be able to get a good job, that perhaps she will not even be permitted to graduate from Ho-Ping. Good God, if I thought I had really done that to her, I don't know what I'd do."

"How did it end? Did you get through to her at all?"

"I don't know. I simply told her that marriage was impossible. That as a priest I had made a sacred promise not to marry."

"Did she accept that, do you think?"

"I don't know. I certainly didn't leave her any room for hope." He was on his feet again, wiping the sweat from his face. He picked up a worry-stone from the desk, weighed it in his hand and then absently put it down again. The room was stifling. I wished he'd let me open the blinds but he hardly seemed to be aware of the heat.

"Look, Vince, don't let yourself concentrate on all the worst possibilities." I was groping for something to solace him. "A lot of it depends on Mei-Lan. I doubt very much that this is all as public as she wants you to believe. Mei-Lan is a very private person; I'd be surprised if she'd been talking very much. I rather suspect that she's using this to get what she wants. Once she accepts the fact that threats aren't going to work I imagine things will calm down." I wasn't sure I believed it but it was the best I could do.

"I hope so." His voice was flat; I wasn't even sure he had heard me. "I have to go," he said, looking at his watch. "It's a long walk home."

"Can't you get a taxi?" It frightened me to think of him walking along those dark roads.

"Probably not at this time of night. They usually don't cruise out this far. Don't worry; I'll be OK, Les." His eyes were full of tears. "You believe me, don't you? You believe that I'd never have done anything . . . ."

"I believe you. Of course, I believe you." I reached up and put my arms around him. We held each other and I could feel him shaking against me. "Vince, it's going to be all right. You have to believe that."

"I'm trying. It's not just for me. It's for Mei-Lan, too. One minute I feel so sorry for her and the next minute I am wild with anger. I don't know what I feel."

"Don't try to figure it out. Wait until you've had a chance to talk to Paul. He's got more experience about these things than you do." I opened the door and he turned toward the stairs.

"Goodnight. Be careful." I kissed him. A sisterly brush against his cheek. As I closed the door I could hear him groping his way down the dark stairway. I went over to the window and opened the blind a little and watched him turn the corner of the building, leaving through the back field so the guard wouldn't see him.

I went into the bathroom and sloshed some cold water on my face and unwrapped the towel from my head. My hair was still wet. It would probably still be wet in the morning and with no electricity I couldn't use a hair dryer. I took off my robe and put on another nightgown–the lightest one I could find–and then I went to sit by the window.

Except for the security lights on the driveway, Ho-Ping was in darkness. Final examinations were finished and most of the boarders were away on school trips or survival training sponsored by the Youth Association. They would return the following week in time for moving-up exercises and graduation. Until then the campus would be largely empty except for the senior boarders who in their privileged status were exempt from any of the training exercises.

I wanted to think but thinking eluded me. Instead I replayed Vincent's anguished account over and over. Looked at with Western eyes it seemed bizarre yet there was another way of seeing in which the images were clear and cohesive. From the beginning Mei-Lan had indicated her need to be a "special girl". She herself had used the phrase. At first it had amused me and then annoyed me but after a while I had accepted it as part of an alien culture. In time I had been lulled into acceptance and ultimately Mei-Lan had achieved her goal: she had become my "special girl". I had offered her a dream, worked out a future for her, promised her opportunities beyond her hopes. I had cast myself in the role of mentor and protector. If I had been asked, I would have said that I was taking her under my wing. In retrospect the image seemed absurdly naive.

About three o'clock a little breeze sprang up. It would have been cooler to stay where I was by the window but the mosquitoes were ferocious and I finally had to crawl under my mosquito net. I slept off and on for what was left of the night, dreaming nightmare dreams, waking up with a start, restlessly seeking for some cool spot for my head. I had forgotten to change my alarm for vacation schedule and it went off with a clang at 6:00. I reached out toward my lamp in the hope that electricity was restored but nothing happened. There was no point in trying to go back to sleep. I felt groggy and my head ached from the heat.

A cold shower helped. I poured a glass of water and peeled an orange and stood eating it over by the window. The bicycle rack was almost empty and I saw no one on the campus except for a few workers engaged in their endless clean-up of the grounds. As I looked I noticed some activity out beyond the school grounds, in the field by the water tower. It was too far away for me to see what was happening but I wondered if the pigs from a nearby farm which sometimes came marauding into the school property had managed to get loose again.

I had just finished dressing and was struggling to do something with my damp hair when there was a knock on the door. I looked at my watch; it wasn't yet seven-thirty. I had no official duties until an English Department meeting at 9:30. Mei-Lan, I thought. It's Mei-Lan. Vincent had said she might try to see me. I dried my hands and wiped my face again. "Coming," I said and started toward the door.

But it was not Mei-Lan; it was someone from administration whom I did not immediately recognize.

"Colonel Sheng see you in his office." She studiously avoided looking at me.

Of course–Colonel Sheng's secretary, the impeccable Miss Shih, she who had summoned me so peremptorily out of class during my first month at Ho-Ping. Then she had looked at me with disdain. Now something else was struggling in her eyes. Fear? Curiosity? A blend of emotions I could not read.

"Please come in," I suggested; "I'll be ready in a minute."

But she shook her head and stood at the open door like a sentinel.

I reached for the belt of my dress and found my hands were shaking. Could Mei-Lan have gone to Colonel Sheng? But why would she? He would have little sympathy for her plight, no doubt blaming her for involving herself with a Westerner in the first place.

I belted my dress and smiled and nodded at Colonel Sheng's secretary. Together we walked across the quadrangle, through the round Door of Perfection and up the stairs to the Security Office. We passed a few teachers along the way but they were from other departments and I barely knew them.

Colonel Sheng's door was open. Everything was as

I remembered it from the day when he had so skillfully humiliated me: the large polished desk, the heavy chair with its classical Chinese carving, the picture of Chiang Kai-Shek in its ornate gilt frame–and Colonel Sheng himself: small, dark, wary, his narrow eyes obscured by heavy, tinted glasses.

Once again he kept me standing despite the chair by the side of his desk. His hands were flat on the desk, his fingers anchoring a rectangular piece of rice paper with Chinese characters. He was perfectly still, not even raising his eyes as I entered. His only movement was an occasional compression of his lips. Finally, he turned the paper and pushed it across the desk toward me.

"Please read," he said, nodding toward it.

"I don't read Mandarin," I explained but my voice was inaudible. For the first time he looked up at me. "I'm sorry," I repeated, doing better this time. "I don't read Mandarin." He reached out for the paper and pulled it toward him.

"Then I will read to you."

He read it in his wretched, stumbling English, while I stood with nothing to support me. Mei-Lan, Beautiful Orchid, was dead. Sometime during the night she had thrown herself from the water tower. Because of her shame, she wrote, she had no course but to commit suicide. She was guilty of wrongful actions and now she was pregnant. She would drink bitterness alone and save her family further disgrace. In the last sentence she named the source of her shame and the father of her child.

Colonel Sheng pushed the paper away and looked directly at me.

CHAPTER XIII

"Li Mei-Lan leave this letter in her pocket," he said. "She address to her family but they show it to me as proper authority." He paused, reaching out and tapping the paper. "Li Mei-Lan mention your name. She say you introduce her to this man and help him to meet her often, even in your house."

I was bathed in perspiration and the room was beginning to tilt. I reached out for the chair beside the desk and sat down but Colonel Sheng was indifferent to my weakness.

"You bring shame to young girl who must drink bitterness alone. You bring shame to Ho-Ping. From beginning I find you bad element." His contempt was palpable.

I heard the words, I saw the disdainful movement of his lips, I saw the dark blunt finger tips which held Mei-Lan's dying letter in place but nothing reached me. I felt neither anger nor fear; my mind was riveted on something else: Vincent. Vincent the father of Mei-Lan's unborn child. I remembered how he had looked, bewildered and frightened, how he had begged me to believe him: "You do believe that I would never do anything . . . ," he had begged and without a moment's hesitation I had put my arms around him, assuring him of my trust.

"We do not wish you at Ho-Ping any longer," Colonel Sheng was saying. "Someone will replace you for final days. Only till tomorrow you stay in your apartment. Then you leave Ho-Ping. You understand?"

I nodded.

"Case of Li Mei-Lan private matter. No need to talk suicide and other matter." He nodded to dismiss me. Clearly he expected no response and I stood and turned toward the door. I hoped I would be able to walk from his office with dignity.

CHAPTER XIV

I met no one as I walked back across the quadrangle. A small black snake lay on the path in the sun but it made no motion to move and I skirted it through the grass. I wondered if it were dead. Ordinarily I would have been terrified but I was remarkably free of fear. I walked up the stairs to my apartment as though I were weightless. I hadn't thought to lock my door or pull down the blinds and now the sun was blazing across the room. I heard a light rumble from the kitchen–the refrigerator. The power must be back on. I filled a pot with water and turned on the electricity. I would have drinking water at last. In my bedroom I hung up my nightgown and made my bed. I'd be able to do something with my hair now, too. I went into the bathroom and took out my hair dryer and a brush.

Only when I faced myself in the mirror did the strange weightless dream burst. My hair hung limply below my ears and my eyes were puffy from too little sleep. I turned off the hair-dryer and unplugged it from the wall. I had no use for it, no use for any of the clutter around me. Mei-Lan, beautiful Mei-Lan was dead and Vincent, she said, was the father of her unborn child.

I unbuckled the belt of my dress and lifted my dress over my head. I kicked off my sandals and lay on my bed in my slip. Mei-Lan. In the darkness she had mounted the narrow ladder that circled the side of the water tower; at the top she had climbed over the safety railing and cast herself down. I could not bear to follow that plummeting body and I put my hands over my eyes as though that would shut it out.

And yet her death was easier to face than the letter she had left. Vincent the father of her child. It wasn't possible. How could it be? How could that anguished recital, those protestations of innocence be false? Not Vincent. And yet . . . . And yet . . . . What other reason could Mei-Lan have for what she had done?

Almost without thought I got up and pulled on a pair of jeans and a T-shirt and went down to get out the Honda. I had to see Vincent. I didn't know what time it was and I had forgotten to put my watch on. It wasn't until I pulled out onto the main highway that I realized I had never driven in the height of the morning traffic before. I kept to the side of the road as much as possible, trying to keep up enough speed to balance me as lorries lumbered past, their ungainly loads shifting dangerously as they rounded the curves. Everything passed me and I was covered with dust and the stifling smell of the exhausts. Motorcycles whirled by, sometimes forcing me off onto the uneven verge. I had forgotten to wear my helmet and with each near miss I wondered when I would go crashing into the muddy ditch that ran along the highway. When finally I turned off the highway onto a dirt road, my fingers were in spasm on the handlebars. Twice I missed the turn leading to the alley where Vincent lived, sloshing through puddles and narrowly avoiding an open drain.

I leaned the Honda against the brick wall and knocked on the back door. I waited a few minutes and knocked again but no one came and when I tried the door, it was locked. I walked around the house, reaching up to try to tap at the windows but there was no response. Stephen, I knew, was up in the mountains for the week. Vincent must already have left for Taipei and perhaps Paul had gone with him. I sat on the steps for a while, waiting. I hardly knew for what. I had used my last remaining energy to get here. I couldn't face the trip back. I thought of leaving the Honda and getting a taxi but that, I knew, was foolish. I had no lock for it and it would be gone within minutes.

Watched curiously by three little moppets I turned the Honda around and started back the way I had come. The trip back was endless, half of it spent behind a local bus which stopped at every intersection; but passing it required more courage than I had at my command. The noon bell was just ringing when I rode into Ho-Ping. The sun was at its most brutal and as soon as I got into my apartment I turned on the water for a shower. But before I could get undressed there was a knock on the door. Surely Colonel Sheng had finished with me. What more could he have to say? Again the knock and before I could get to the door the handle began to turn. I stood where I was. I didn't have the energy for another encounter. The door opened slowly, "Leslie?" a Chinese voice called. "May I come in?"

"Madame Hsu!" I stood up. Even now that voice could call me to attention.

"Forgive me. I tried to telephone but there was no answer."

I was suddenly aware of how unkempt I looked–my wet T-shirt, my limp hair, my scruffy sandals. Madame Hsu, of course, was her impeccable self. "Please sit down."

I pulled a chair out of the sun and rearranged the blind. "I'm afraid I can't offer you anything to drink. I just boiled some water but it's still hot. We haven't had any refrigeration until just today."

She shook her head. "It doesn't matter. Perhaps afterwards we can go and have some lunch but now I want to talk to you." She was looking at me appraisingly. "Colonel Sheng saw you this morning, I believe."

I nodded. There had been times when Madame Hsu's control had infuriated me but now it calmed me. That hard imperious expression had softened and she looked as I had remembered her the day she had taken me to her apartment–a woman marked by suffering but who had not been cowed.

"Leslie, I know about Mei-Lan. Not simply about her suicide–that, of course, will be common knowledge. Colonel Sheng cannot control that. But I know also about the accusation she has brought against your friend Father Vincent."

"I went to see him this morning. That's where I was when you telephoned. But he wasn't home. No one was home."

"You went to tell him about Mei-Lan, of course. There is no way he could know so soon."

"I had to see him. Vincent was here last night. He and Mei-Lan had had a terrible misunderstanding. She expected him to . . . to . . . ." I stumbled over the sentence.

"She expected him to marry her and, of course, he couldn't." Madame Hsu said it so evenly that it dissipated some of the horror.

"Leslie, you must believe what I am going to tell you now. You must believe it for your own sake and for Father Vincent's. Mei-Lan was not pregnant. I am sure of that."

"But . . . ." I tried to interrupt.

She raised her hand. "Please let me finish. When Mei-

Lan first came to Ho-Ping I was her teacher. She had lost her mother the year before and her father was already planning to remarry. Mei-Lan, I noticed, often looked lonely and a little frightened. I especially noticed that during her monthly periods she seemed in unusual pain. I hesitated to interfere with her family life but I felt it was essential that she receive some medical help and with the approval of our principal I made an appointment for Mei-Lan to see a doctor.

"From the beginning he was concerned about her condition and he called me as soon as he had the result of the tests he had ordered. Mei-Lan, he explained, had a condition called in English, I believe, endometriosis. This would account for her painful periods as well as for abnormal bleeding. The most serious consequence of the disease, however, is infertility. Dr. Liang was quite direct in explaining that while he could lessen her periods of pain he doubted that Mei-Lan would ever be able to bear a child.

"At first I thought it would be better not to tell her, to wait until she was older but Dr. Liang did not agree. 'Nothing is gained by escaping from the truth,' he said and in the end I knew he was right.

"Mei-Lan said very little when we told her. Perhaps she was still too young to understand the full consequences. She asked only that we not tell her father for whom it would be a loss of face."

We sat in silence for a long time. "So she lied. Vincent isn't . . . ." Once again I found it hard to finish the sentence.

"No. Vincent isn't the father of Mei-Lan's child. There

was no child."

I didn't know I was crying until I tasted the salt on my lips. Through the blur of my tears Madame Hsu's face looked softer, almost compassionate. I wished she would put her arms around me. I needed someone to help me keep all the pieces from flying apart.

"I think you were very fond of Mei-Lan. You wanted to give her good things, things she could never have achieved on her own. She was ambitious and you admired this in her but I don't think you realized how deep it went and how vital it was to Mei-Lan's pride to realize her dream. Then you introduced her to your good friend Father Vincent–another way to make her special–and he followed along, asking her help, thanking her, singling her out."

I started to speak but she stopped me again.

"No, let me finish, Leslie. Then the dream you had offered didn't come true. The scholarship from America didn't materialize. Very casually you said, maybe next year. But for Mei-Lan it was as though you had broken a promise.

"Then one day, when she least expected it, Father Vincent told her he would have to postpone her baptism. He had, no doubt, begun to question her sincerity–or her understanding. But for Mei-Lan his decision must have been staggering. She had studied her lessons, she had performed creditably and then with no explanation that she could understand she was told that she had failed."

"Did she really want baptism so much?"

"There is no way to tell. It was, at least, a sign for her, a symbol of a way of life that she hungered for. And, of course, it was also, she thought, a way to please Father

Vincent. That it would turn just the reverse she could not have foreseen."

"But to think that he would marry her . . . ."

"That is the most difficult of all, but I must remind you that in our culture those marks of friendship which you employ so casually are interpreted more seriously. I'm sure you remember poor Miss Gao whom you championed so resolutely. So it is possible, I think, that Mei-Lan expected marriage. Whatever she expected, it was powerful enough to lead to her death."

"But what good did it do? She was so young, so beautiful, so bright. She had everything to live for."

Madame Hsu smiled. "Spoken like a true American. But I'm afraid that was not Mei-Lan's vision. She saw it very differently."

"But to commit suicide. What good could that do? It didn't change anything for her."

"Oh, but it did. It succeeded in destroying the two people who had betrayed her. Had you never noticed what strong passions jealousy and revenge were in Mei-Lan?"

Of course I had noticed but in my innocence I thought they were words, paper emotions, used in a moment of anger and then forgotten. But for Mei-Lan they were blood and bone.

I felt too tired to talk any more. "You tried to tell me, didn't you? You tried to warn me that I didn't really understand."

"I wanted to save you from disappointment if I could."

"You seemed so harsh sometimes, so cruel and implacable."

"Kill the tiger, save the cub."

I looked at her questioningly.

"It means to wound in order to save life."

"Does it always work like that?"

"Not always. Sometimes the pain is too great and even the cub does not survive."

I thought of her brother, that dark, skeletal figure in his airless room and wondered if she were thinking of him, too. I felt that I should thank her for what she had tried to do but I wasn't ready for that yet. Madame Hsu had turned her chair and was looking around at the room. "What are you going to do now, Leslie?"

The question came as a shock. I hadn't given a thought to anything beyond seeing Vincent. Now I realized that Colonel Sheng's ultimatum gave me very little choice.

"I have to be out of here by tomorrow morning. Colonel Sheng's final word."

" Where will you go?" she asked.

"I don't know. I have to talk to Vincent and let him know about Mei-Lan. There's no way he could know what's happened. The house was all closed up when I went over there this morning. Vincent said last night that Father Paul wanted him to get out of here. He probably went to Taipei. Maybe Father Paul went with him."

"Do you have the Taipei number?"

CHAPTER XIV

"Some place." I rummaged around on my desk finally handing a slip of paper to Madame Hsu. The cook answered at once and I sat listening while the conversation went on in Mandarin.

"Both Vincent and Father Paul have gone up to the bamboo forest at Shitou," she explained as she hung up. "They expect to stay for a few days. But the cook gave me an emergency number where they can be reached. Shall I call?"

I nodded, wondering how I could ever tell Vincent what had happened. But I was lucky. It was Father Paul who answered. Vince was out taking a walk, he explained.

"Are you OK, Leslie? Vincent was afraid that Mei-Lan would turn up at your door. She threatened to go to the authorities. I hope she didn't . . . ."

I interrupted him before he could go on. "Paul," I said hesitating . . . and then the sentence was out. "Mei-Lan is dead. She committed suicide."

I could hear his intake of breath but for a minute he said nothing and then a single monosyllable, "How?"

"She jumped from the water tower."

Again that silence. And then almost a sob. "My God!"

Suddenly I had no breath and I handed the phone to Madame Hsu. I hardly heard what they were saying. The beating of my heart was like claps of thunder. It was as though at that moment the realization of what had happened had finally reached me.

"My God, Leslie. I can't believe it. How did you find out?" Paul asked as I took the phone.

"Colonel Sheng. Mei-Lan left a letter for her family which they shared with Colonel Sheng. He sent for me this morning and read me the letter. It's very clear. She names Vincent as the father of her child. He told me I had to be out of Ho-Ping by tomorrow morning. I think he's trying to keep it quiet for the sake of the school."

Paul was silent for a minute and then he asked:, "Have you made plans, Leslie? I'm sure you'll want to go back to the States but it will take a couple of days at least to get your papers in order. I hope you will consider staying with us in Taipei as long as you need."

"Thank you. I'd be grateful for that and it would give me a chance to talk to Vincent."

Paul hesitated. "I think I'm going to suggest that Vincent stay on at Shitou for a few more days until we can figure out what we should do. It's out of the way and there's less chance of his meeting people who know him. I doubt if Colonel Sheng will be able to keep this quiet for long."

By the time we hung up it had been arranged that I would take the late afternoon train up to Taipei. Paul would meet me at the station. Ordinarily the process of leaving Taiwan would have taken days of red tape, with visits to the immigration office, forms to be filled out and affixed with the school seal but in this Colonel Sheng was my benefactor. He had already begun the process of obtaining my exit visa.

Were it not for Madame Hsu I would never have been ready to leave Ho-Ping. She helped me lug my suitcases from the storage room and stood patiently while I tried to make decisions. "Leslie, take only what you really want. The rest I will take care of." And when I stood in a hopeless muddle of indecision, she made the choices for me. Some time early in the afternoon she went over to the school cafeteria and came back with the inevitable rice boxes packed with chicken and cabbage. We ate them standing in the chaos of my apartment.

At exactly four o'clock we loaded my two suitcases into the waiting taxi and started for the train station. As we drove through the entrance gates I waved to my old friend the custodian. But this time there was no answering smile. Perhaps it was he who had discovered the body and I wondered what else he knew. Now he sat unmoving, staring past the taxi like one of those ancient images I had seen in Tainan.

My trip up to Taipei was a reversal of my trip south ten months earlier. The same hard seats, the same lukewarm tea served by the efficient, uniformed attendant. The book I had brought to pass the time lay unopened. I was overcome with a fatigue the other side of sleep. Father Paul, with a taxi waiting, waved to me from the restricted area outside the station. We talked very little along the way; he seemed as reluctant as I. Bryan welcomed us at the door, a little thinner than I remembered and with a less healthy pallor.

"And this is our newcomer, Adam," Paul announced nodding toward a slight young man who acknowledged me with a bow but did not smile. "Adam is originally from Thailand but he has volunteered to help us out during his summer vacation." Again that studied nod. Adam, clearly, was not one to give anything away.

I went to bed almost at once in the same airless little room I had used nearly a year earlier. This time I was less disturbed by the noisy conversations, the night-long radio, the early morning crow of the roosters. Bryan and Adam were out of the house by the time I was washed and dressed. Paul sat with me while I ate my breakfast. It was the first chance we had had to talk and I could feel his anxiety. He pushed my bowl and mug out of the way and sat back with his arms crossed.

"I haven't said anything to Bryan or Adam," he began, "although they are certainly aware that something is up." He sighed. "I want to talk to you first and see if you can throw some more light on what's happened." Another long pause. "Of course Vincent and I talked on Thursday night after he had seen you but he was beyond himself. I think he still hoped that he might be able to calm Mei-Lan, make her understand that marriage was simply not possible." He sighed. "I don't think the rest of this ever entered his mind. Did she say anything to you, anything about being pregnant?"

I shook my head. "I never saw her at all. I guess I thought it might blow over. I thought if I talked to Mei-Lan that maybe I could . . . ." But suddenly I could not go on. Colonel Sheng's voice was in my ears, his hard Chinese accent reciting the assertion of Mei-Lan's pregnancy. "From the beginning I found you bad element," he was saying. "You bring shame to young girl who must drink bitterness alone."

I cried then with a passion I had not felt before. Perhaps we were "bad elements" full of our Western dreams and ambitions. Paul made no effort to console me. He let me work it out–half crying, half explaining. When finally I was able to sit back in my chair he said, "I know, Leslie, that it would be a lot better for you to talk to Vincent face to face but I don't think it's wise to bring him back here just now. See what you can manage on the telephone. He knows most of what has happened. He knows about Mei-Lan's suicide and her accusation of pregnancy. What he does not know is Madame Hsu's explanation that in fact Mei-Lan cannot have been pregnant. That is something I have left for you to explain."

I spoke to Vincent early that afternoon. I don't know what I expected but Vincent's responses unnerved me. I found him reduced to monosyllables. He responded to my recital almost without emotion. He thanked me. He asked me about my plans to return home. He hoped that I would recover from these difficult days. He wished me well for my future. We said goodbye like two well-wishing acquaintances.

Two days later my exit papers came through and I made my reservations for New York, flying direct from Taipei to Kennedy Airport. Tom was waiting for me at Customs but except for an appraising look he said nothing about my arrival two weeks earlier than I had been expected. We had a festive welcome-home dinner that night as I explained that school was really over except for the final exercises and lots of the foreign teachers leave early to avoid the summer heat.

For the first twenty-four hours my parents were satisfied that I was just very tired. After that it was clear to them that something was wrong. They waited patiently as they always had. Only Tom forced my silence, following me out into the garden, taking me by the shoulders and turning me toward him.

"Don't, Tom, please don't. Not now." It was the first time I had cried since I was home.

"Then when?"

"Someday. Soon. When I can. OK?"

But even as I said it I wondered if there would ever be a day when I could. How could I explain? And even more: how could they understand? How could I explain Mei-Lan? Or Vincent? Or myself? How could I explain what had taken place in another language, another world? Perhaps later after Vincent and I had been in touch, perhaps then I'd be able to talk.

Two weeks after I returned home a letter came from Taipei. The envelope was typed and I was sure it must be from Vincent. But when I opened it, it was in Paul's meticulous hand. He was sorry to bring me more bad news, he began. Vincent had been in a very serious motorcyle accident. He had returned from Shitou two days after I had left. That night he stayed in Taipei and the next day they had both taken the train to Chi-Yi. The decision had been made to close the mission and they wanted to sell the house as soon as possible.

It was dark when they arrived but they were lucky to find a taxi willing to take them out to their house. The lights were on and as they pulled up they saw Bryan coming to open the door. Vincent waved as he crossed the alley with his suitcase. Then, without a second's warning, a motorcycle came out of nowhere and headed straight for him. It was a large powerful machine manned by two young men with their faces partially covered. Everyone saw it and a couple of people screamed a warning but Vincent didn't have a chance. The motorcycle, of course, disappeared immediately.

It took a while to get an ambulance as it always does and

CHAPTER XIV

Vincent didn't regain consciousness. Paul did his best to get a couple of bystanders to tell the police that they had witnessed the accident but, of course, when the chips are down, everybody slinks away. The police have promised to investigate but we know what that means.

As I read Paul's letter I remembered that I had seen that motorcycle–sleek and black and powerful. "My two brother let me use their motorcycle," Mei-Lan had told me proudly and I had watched her, small but sure and masterful, as she had maneuvered it out of Ho-Ping and onto the highway. I needed no reports from witnesses or the police. The cause of Vincent's "accident" was patently clear.

Vincent is now in the clinic, Paul's letter continued. He has regained consciousness and the doctors are pleased with his progress. However, his legs are very badly crushed and the doctors here are offering little hope that he will be able to walk again. Paul is making arrangements to fly him back to the States as soon as his condition has stabilized sufficiently. Whatever the future holds he should be back in his own country.

In the light of these events, Paul explained, it has seemed better to close up the mission at Chi-Yi immediately. They have put the house in the care of a Catholic family who has promised to try to sell it for them. Remarkably enough, Ho-Ping seems not to have suffered. Colonel Sheng has succeeded in keeping the incidents contained so that the reputation of the school has not been injured.

In fact, the registration for the summer session is full and they have already begun to advertise for Western teachers for the coming year.